GHOST TRACKS

STORIES OF PITTSBURGH PAST

by

MARK SABA

ISBN: 978-1-945917-16-5

Printed in the United States of America

Cover Design: Mark Saba
Cover Photo: Jack Delano
Author Photo: Nick Saba

Some of the stories in *Ghost Tracks* were previously published:

"That Hill," "Asthma," "Raquel and I," "The Magnolia Branch," "National Biscuit Company," and "Tracings" — *The Folio Club*
"The Magnolia Branch" — *Cargoes* (of Hollins University)
"View" — *Litro*
"Eva" — *Phantasmagoria*

Also by Mark Saba:

Calling the Names
The Landscapes of Pater
Painting a Disappearing Canvas
Tipping Points
Signs
The Shoemaker
Letters from Novosibirsk

"Making other books jealous since 2004"

Big Table Publishing Company
Boston, MA
www.bigtablepublishing.com

in memory of my mother
Lorraine Kubiak

Table of Contents

"Everything is, everything exists, only because I love."
~ Leo Tolstoy

I
INNOCENCE

That Hill

That hill. What was it about that hill?

It was a hill that made his heart jump, a yellow brick that seemed too bright for cars and buses. Too clean.

Today is a day for a dreamsicle, a quarter in his hand, a walk up the long, long hill up from his grandparents' house and up to the flatter road, then on to that hill. He doesn't often walk up that hill; he usually only sees it from the back window of their car.

But today he is walking with his sister Katie and yes they are going to walk up that clean bright hill. At the top there is a movie theater. Halfway up there is an ice cream store. But they will not go there, she says; they will go instead to the top and around the bend. There will be another store and that's where all the dreamsicles are. He usually doesn't want a dreamsicle but today he does.

They are going up. He watches the bricks and they are not really as clean as they look from the car window. There is a bit of paper here and there and tired looking grass every few bricks, and big oily spots. But there is ice cream at the top and now ice cream in a big store halfway up and they're not stopping there.

Katie has a loud voice. Sometimes he thinks it is louder than his mother's or his grandmother's. Now it is very loud as she explains to him that *they just don't sell dreamsicles in the big ice cream store*. They are passing it anyway and there is the yellow hill beside him.

A wide blue car is coming down, turning into the ice cream store which is really a milk store because Katie just said so. And she can read, or else she pretends to which is what he really thinks. But he doesn't like to fight with her when there's something to look at. The road.

But soon he has to think about breathing instead because Katie walks fast. And it's summer and sometimes in summer you can't breathe because the air is full of steam.

"Wait."

They're already at the top. Come on, come on, says Katie, but no he will stand right there and not talk but breathe.

Below them is the hill now, coming right up to their feet and to Katie's twisted up face. God will get her for making those faces. Standing above the yellow road which isn't yellow anymore, but brown or red.

There are hills far back. They are hills against the sky that is faintly blue and the hills gray. A little smoke comes up behind them—between him and the hills comes the yellow road turning brown or red, the old red school, black and gray and green rooftops, buses and streetcars. But he doesn't see any of this; he only knows he must look at it while Katie pulls him by the shoulder. He will not know or see it for many years. After twenty years he will slowly come to see it, while living in a similar land very far away.

Later they are on the streetcar. He, his sister, and his mother. His mother is sitting quietly the way she usually sits; Katie is asking her things and sometimes she answers Katie. But he has a big seat to himself. He has already looked at all the faces riding with them. Now it is time to look out the window. There are other hills—they go up and down and the streetcar goes back and forth. He doesn't see the hills; he feels them because the streetcar feels them and he is with the streetcar.

Every single day he wishes he could ride a streetcar. On the streetcar he doesn't feel like talking. When his mother talks to him he hears her but he doesn't turn his head; he doesn't talk. He'd rather say something to the people outside the window, and they can't hear him.

12

Some stores go down and then come up again; then he is thrown back a little on the seat and he has to hold on. Sometimes a pigeon flies along with the streetcar; sometimes it is gray and purple or brown and white and one time is was mostly white. That was a good pigeon to see.

Then there is a pizza store with a little green man holding up a big circle pizza, with brown dots on it. Once he saw a big dark sky, and thunder he could hear, and smell. On a hill way out is a line of tall crosses, a place to put people after they die. And there is a place to put fire engines, a place to put a lot of cars, a place where grandfathers go that has dark windows and pink lights like worms, a place where his mother has a friend and they go to visit her.

Balls roll down streets after people lose them. If they are big speckled balls you can see them but if you're in a streetcar you can't get them.

Once when the streetcar stops there is a pet store. Now he will tell her he wants a parakeet. Like Lois next door has, but not that color. One that's blue. He'll tell her. Not now, after the streetcar ride. He'll teach it to talk. To say shut up hello I want some pizza and ice cream.

But there is where the doctor is. He doesn't like the doctor with the cold hands and bald head that gives him shots every week. He smells like new clothes. New clothes are bad to smell and wear. It's bad to get them new on Christmas morning instead of toys.

There's the place where all the new cars are parked with big price tags in their windows. New cars are good to smell. Candles are good to smell too and there they are in the window with statues of church people. Church people don't live, but you can look at them and look at them until their faces shine. And the man with the big voice starts talking all around you. Everyone gets up and sits down and then again.

There's an older boy on a red bike like he'll have. He's going so fast he's bending down and passing up the streetcar because it stopped. Another grandmother is getting off slow. Nobody is saying anything until she is off and holding a bag hanging down her arm. She is walking away a grandmother like his down the new hill with big ugly

13

toes coming out the front of her shoes like his grandmother's, who smells good.

It's okay to close your eyes if you feel the sun. The streetcar's going around a bend now with the sun on it.

She wakes him. The streetcar man is waiting for them to get off. He's not friendly from behind but then he is if he turns around.

The ground feels moving. She has to use his hand to go across the street. Across the street where his father is sitting in the goodsmelling car with candy, waiting.

Asthma

The room was now green, like the little wormy crab apples he and Will picked off the ground at the edge of the woods, bit into once, then threw as far as they could down the hill. He spent a lot of time in that room, his brother and sister at school, mother trudging up and down the stairs with armfuls of laundry, cleaning supplies, and ginger ale for him to drink. She let him stay in bed, but he didn't much like it, because it reminded him of not sleeping and the dark, and that dry taste in his mouth. Her friend, Frank, had painted his room just before Christmas. It was now apple-green. Before that it had been blue like the Blessed Mother.

Frank had a loud voice, or maybe it was the case that all men did, and Luke was not used to hearing a man's voice in his house. Frank was loud, but didn't talk much—just smile, especially when talking to his mother.

From the apple-green room Luke went directly to the bathroom for a drink of water, coughing only once along the way. The morning feeling in him was hollow, as if a tornado had blown inside him during the night and left nothing but a bruised windpipe through which he had to breathe. Breathing was painful, something he'd rather not do, but water and ginger ale could take away the burning for a minute or two.

He looked in the mirror and saw sad eyes, though he did not feel sad. They were half-closed eyes, surrounded by gray. His hair was tasseled and his skin looked like pie dough. The only thing that felt

15

good right now was his soft pajamas. On the way back to his room he heard the floor register begin to rattle, and knew he could warm up his feet by standing over it and letting the burnt-smelling furnace air blow through him. While standing there, seeing how long he could take it before the grate burned his feet, he looked through the window and saw a gray sky, and the first few snowflakes of the season blowing back and forth. Today was the day he had to go to the hospital. Maybe they would have chocolate pudding there, as there was rumored to be, and television through all hours of the night.

She didn't say much during the drive. He watched the clouds billow up from behind the hills until they passed the steel mill, with its own thick, yellow-and-orange cloud maker. Driving along the mill made the car feel a little colder, because it blocked the light, but he liked watching the jets of flame against the uneven black silhouette. It made him feel important, and forget his coughing.

He recognized the hospital, because he had just seen his grandfather there during the summer, waving from one of the windows in his undershirt and back brace. He looked up to that same window now, and found it bare. All of its windows were closed, because winter was already here and all the sick people must be cold.

Come on honey, she said, helping him out of the car like she never did. It was a busy street for a hospital to be on: the City. She carried his bag and held his hand very firmly. Inside, the place was full of nuns. There was an old one sitting at a fancy table when you came in, and she gave him a lollipop. Her teeth were yellow when she smiled.

Dr. Stendhal came around to check on him in his room: it was green around the bottom and white around the top, and there were three beds against each of two opposite walls. Dr. Stendhal still had that scary, clean smell, even outside his office. He listened to Luke's lungs and told him to breathe and breathe. But there was no coughing now. Next he asked Luke's mother to step out into the hallway so they could whisper. That's what people did most often in hospitals:

whisper. After the doctor left it was time for his mother to go. She looked away while hugging him, and said she would say a prayer for him before she went to bed.

He smelled dinner before it came, but could not figure out what it was by the way it smelled. A nurse brought it in on a tray, but he still couldn't tell what it was because it was all covered up with upside-down pie pans. She set it on the little table that was attached to the side of the bed and swung over in front of him, and uncovered the biggest pan. What he saw was a bowl of green vomit.

"What is this?" he gasped.

"Pea soup. It's good, sweetie. Try some."

"Could I have some buttered noodles, please?"

"No-no. You're on a liquid diet."

"What's that mean?"

"It means you can only have liquid things—like soups, juices, you know. *Liquids.*"

For the first time since coming to the hospital now he began to cough, a long uncontrollable cough that reminded him of the burning in his throat. He went for the Jello.

"Nu (cough)— Nu (cough)— Nurse?"

"Yes, sweetheart?"

"I guess I could have a milk shake then? (cough)"

"What a smart kid you are! I'll see what I can do about that for tomorrow. Just try the soup for now, though. It's real good. I'm not a nurse honey. Your nurse will be coming in soon. Bye!"

There was another liquid, brown, in a smaller bowl which he dared not try, and a glass of milk which tasted like milk anywhere, but he didn't feel like finishing it. It was the first time he could remember having lost his appetite. He set his mind on finding the television instead. The room was even bigger without his mother and Dr. Stendhal in it. The other beds gleamed at him with their stiff white sheets and pillows. The floor (also green and white) was shiny too. Each of the six beds had a little swinging table and another table with a lamp beside it. There was a big, bright window with green drapes

17

opened on either side of it, and a lingering Dr. Stendhal smell. No television.

"Hello."

Luke turned back to the doorway. A real nurse stood there, holding a white torpedo upside-down in the air.

"Hi (cough). What's that?"

"Turn around. This'll be quick."

"But—"

"No buts here, except one—ha, ha."

She pulled down his pajama bottoms and dabbed his behind with something cool. Then the needle went in, and she kept it in for a very long time. He didn't flinch, but refused to say anything to her, even when she asked if he needed anything.

"And oh," she added as she was leaving, "the T.V.'s in the next room down the hall to the right. You may watch it until eight o'clock. Then it's bed time for you."

He did finally look up at her, but not for long. She was pretty.

The soreness from the torpedo shot was nearly gone as he approached the T.V. room. He was hardly coughing at all in this hospital, and wondered if he had to live there if he wanted to stop coughing for good. The hallway was cool and dim, but he noticed the familiar flickering very soon, and then the voice of Granny on *The Beverly Hillbillies*.

The room was much smaller than he'd imagined it. There were an old couch and a couple of hard-looking chairs, a round, gray rug, and some very beat-up wooden trucks. On the couch sat a fat woman beside a little girl who had a tube sticking out of her arm and leading up to a plastic bag on stilts. In one of the chairs, to the left of the couch, sat a mean-looking teenager with red marks all over his face and big feet. He too was in his pajamas, but no slippers.

"Hi," Luke said, taking the other uncomfortable chair at first, then slipping down to the ugly rug.

The fat woman smiled at him and the mean kid said nothing. But Luke lost himself in the T.V. show, and even laughed a little, though this set him off, and he lapsed into a long coughing fit.

In what seemed to be less than a second that nurse appeared in the hallway, holding her hands on her hips and looking at him the way the school principal might.

"Why don't you come back to the room," she said. He knew it was not a request. He waved to the T.V. room people and the fat lady smiled again. The mean kid nodded. The Beverly Hillbillies were waving goodbye too, the way they always did at the end of the show.

"Do I need to have another shot?" he said to her.

"No, not tonight."

She led him back into this room, where a nun stood waiting by his bed, holding a tall glass of some terrible, colorless liquid.

"Thank you, Sister," the nurse said. "I'll take that."

The nun folded her arms and mumbled a short prayer. Then she blessed herself and touched Luke's forehead with her old hand, before quietly leaving. He looked up at the nurse, who stood ready to tuck him in.

"Do I have to drink that now?"

"If you want to."

"I think I'll wait till later," he added quickly, before she could change her mind.

"Good night, dear."

She brought the cardboard sheets up to his chest and tucked them into the sides, raised the metal bars, and turned off the brightest light. He waited until she'd left before daring to look at the strange liquid, which made the glass sweat beads of water. It was funny to see a straw sticking out of all that medicine. Just as he was planning to carry it down to the bathroom and empty it into the toilet, a doctor passed by in the hallway, looking straight at him. They were everywhere, and they would know if he didn't drink it.

In the next moment, then, he sat up, picked up the glass, closed his eyes, and tried to hold his breath while drinking, so that he wouldn't taste it. But he was not very successful, and the soothing flavor of vanilla milk shake slid down his throat. He drank as much as he could before they could discover their mistake.

He opened his eyes to the morning, feeling that he might have slept and he might not have: the burning was in his throat, and he remembered someone giving him water once or twice during the night. That's what he wanted now. He pulled off the stale covers; his feet hit the cold green floor. Cool air swirled in the hallway as he walked to the lavatory.

When he came back to his room he found it was no longer his. Someone was moving in beside him. The big drape was closed around the next bed, and he heard loud voices coming from behind it, using a lot of words he never heard before. But more interesting was the tray that was now by his bed. It had a small bowl of hot cereal on it, a glass of juice, and another small bowl with something brown and mushy in it.

The cereal was something his mother had made him before, only soggier. But he ate it, and drank the orange juice. The brown mush he left untouched.

"Hey, kiddo."

He looked over; the curtain had been drawn, and all the people had left but the one lying in bed. It was a man, or at least a boy old enough to shave and maybe go to college. One of his legs was held up by strings in the air. It was covered in white strips, like a mummy.

"What happened to you?" Luke said.

"I had a little accident."

"Wow. That's neat. It looks like Halloween. Does it hurt?"

"It did. But now I don't feel much of anything." He pointed to the medicine bag on stilts that fed into his arm. "What are you in for?"

"I can't breathe."

"You're fooling me."

"It's called brown key-hole azma. Yesterday they gave me a shot that was as long as your foot."

20

"How long you stayin'?"

"Three days. My mom's coming to visit though. Is your mom coming too?"

"She was just here."

"How about your dad?"

The man put one arm behind his head and looked to the window:

"Him? Nah, you won't be meeting him. He's probably drunk right now."

"My dad's dead."

He turned back to look at Luke.

"Oh? How?"

"I don't know. He just died. When I was little." Now Luke noticed the bruises on the man's face, on the side that had been turned away from him. He didn't say anything about them, because they looked scary. "What's your name?" he finally said.

"Kevin."

"Kevin?"

"Don't wear it out."

"Do you want to finish my breakfast?"

Kevin liked to sleep, Luke figured out, even more than eating, because he didn't have anything to eat all morning. Any time Luke looked over he saw Kevin's eyes were closed. But other things happened that day to keep Luke occupied.

There were more shots, of course. Big ones and little ones, all over his behind. But they were helping him to stop coughing, and most of the nurses were nice. One even smelled good. Dr. Stendhal came once, right after breakfast, with his usual cold hands and scary smell. He made Luke breathe deep and this made him cough—he knew it would—but the coughing didn't last long. Luke asked if he could have a hot dog and this even got the old man to smile, though the answer was no.

Next came his mother, and she sat in the chair by his bed so they could play cards. He could tell she didn't like the hospital either,

21

because she spent a lot of time looking lost. She was never like that at home. They had lunch together (brown soup without noodles) and he found himself falling asleep as she rubbed his back. When he awoke from his nap she was gone, but she had left a package on his bed. Inside it was a set of matchbox cars, each in its own little yellow box. He immediately set to driving them along the hills and folds of his sheets.

An uncle of his stopped by on his way home from work: Uncle Norman. Uncle Norman had thin blonde hair and big glasses, and he brought Luke a Creepy Crawler set. It was one of the best gifts he'd ever gotten. Uncle Norman smiled a lot, and asked Luke everything there was to ask about his stay there, and how he felt, and whether or not the food was good. Luke was a little sad after he left.

Soon, though, his mother returned, this time with his sister and brother. He let his brother play with the cars but his sister just kept saying that she didn't like it there and wanted to leave. She was still wearing her school clothes. When his mother stepped out to the hallway to talk with a nurse he told her about the milk shakes, and that he was already getting sick of them, there were so many.

"Get to sleep now, Luke. The doctor says you're getting better. Tomorrow you're coming home." His mother gathered the children and gave him a little kiss. Then she was gone again.

Luke fell asleep coughing only once or twice, and wondering about a lot of things: about why the pea soup, why the funny roommate, why his mother didn't keep the puppy his aunt had given them, and why he didn't really miss home the first night but now he did. He awoke a couple of times that night, but not from coughing. He woke up hearing voices in the hall, trying to shut them out so he could go back to sleep.

Another time, when he awoke, he found that the bed opposite his was no longer empty. In it lay another sleeping boy, an old boy with a thick bandage around his head. He was sleeping very deeply, and around his bed sat a group of crying women. Luke drifted in and out of sleep for the rest of that night, hearing more voices, seeing white coats flashing by and standing around that bed, and watching the women hug one another. By morning light the boy and the women were gone. The bed lay there fresh and white, as if nothing had happened, though one of the chairs beside the bed was still crooked where the largest, babushka-wearing woman had been.

And that morning felt strange for Luke. It felt like a morning long ago for him, though he could not find it, it was so buried in his head. He barely ate his breakfast, which seemed the worst yet. Kevin had left his bed to go for a little ride in the rolling chair. Luke didn't like being alone now; he didn't like the bright light coming in through the window, or the way the sheets smelled, or even the Creepy Crawler set. He fell back into the bed and pulled the sheet and heavy blanket up to his neck, but this still did not take away his feeling. *Where did that boy go? Why were those women crying? Did his mother come to get him?* Now he had to cough, but he held it back. He lay very still and wouldn't cough, no matter what.

Dr. Stendhal came, even colder than usual, and smelling worse than the sheets. He didn't say very much to Luke, but told the nurse to write things down on a pad, which he then signed. After they left a nun came, this time a young smiling one, and she gave Luke a little coloring book with prayers in it. He was beginning to feel like getting out from under the covers now, and just then his mother came.

They passed the mill again on the way home, but there wasn't much smoke coming out of it that day. Luke felt happy in the car with the sun warming him up through the window. But his mother was very quiet. Wasn't she happy that he was coming home?

At home she had a surprise for him: the fried noodles-and-potato dough his grandmother sometimes made. It was his favorite thing. He asked if he had to go to school now and she said no. She said that when he went to school the next day he would be able to get up and walk to the water fountain in the hallway any time he wanted if he was coughing. She had spoken with Sister DeLellus about it.

Luke looked out the back window to their yard, which was all brown and orange-red now. Everything had died there. He smelled lunch cooking, and started thinking about the wonderful taste of *pyzy* in his mouth, as the furnace kicked on and his mother came up behind him to give him one, long hug.

"What's wrong?" he said to her.

"Nothing," she answered. "Just nothing."

Birds

In cages 3, 6, and 10 the birds are all doing fine. Dot says the singing sometimes comes over the whole house. She might even close the cellar door while she does her cross-words, so she can think. How many cross-words can a woman do anyway?

Most of my workbench is full of canaries now. I used to have parakeets too, years back. But they squawk too much, especially when they have company. Canaries get a better price. People seem to like the orange and brown ones. Dot still prefers the yellow.

In a few of the other cages, 5 and 8 to be exact, the birds are shy and mostly quiet. They're not unhealthy, just females. Some people prefer birds that don't sing much. But those birds, I catch their eyes from time to time. I see they're watching me.

I been at the mill for almost forty years now. Some of the guys been there longer. It's like my second home. I don't know if when I retire I'll be able to handle it—being cooped up in our house all day. I might even miss the bus rides, since I can doze off, or think, when I ride. It's about the only free time I can get.

Thank God for hunting. The twelve-pointer I got last year had everyone in a tizzy. I kept the head and mounted him for our basement game room. I love it hanging down there; it makes me remember that feeling of getting him—POW—right through the chest.

Last year is when I had Nevermore, my crow. He had fallen too far from the nest, and looked injured. What the hell, I brought him home. Dot almost started in on me, but I could see she thought he was cute.

Nevermore lived on the back porch, just hopping around at first, which was all he could do. He ate just about anything, but liked the hard-boiled egg mixture I make for my chicks too. He also liked shiny things, like coins and my daughters' hair pins. He'd hide them in the gutter after he started to fly. He hung around all summer and fall, flying around the neighborhood and always coming back to sit on our block wall. He could even say his name, and would repeat it if he was looking for something to eat—*Nevermore, Nevermore*—until one of us brought him a slice of apple or raisins. When it got cold he took off, and we never seen him again.

I grew up next door, in a house my dad built onto a log cabin that was already there. When I got older I bought the next lot, and built my house there. It's a little thing, but it holds the four kids, my wife, and me just fine. My older sister took over my dad's house; she married and had four of her own long before I had mine. Then her husband left her, and she got to be bitter and quiet. What can I do? People don't even believe we're related sometimes.

Dot and I always have the Christmas party. We invite a lot of the neighborhood, and Dot's sisters come up from town. We go through five cases of beer every year.

My oldest girl, Sissy, went to New York with a friend who wanted to be a model. Well, her friend didn't get the job but wouldn't you know it, Sissy did. They dyed her hair and gave her a bunch of fancy clothes and changed her name to *Sofia*. Je-sus Christ, can you believe it? I can tell you one thing: I will never call her Sofia as long as I live. She is making good money though.

Here's the thing about that damn steel mill: it gets under your skin. You can't wash it away. You'll dream about it, taste it, breathe it even when the flowers are blooming. You got to think of it as a good paycheck, and that's all.

Now the air is a lot better than it was when I was a kid, when they had the streetlights on all afternoon so you could see where you were going. From the top of Mount Washington, where you can see all of Pittsburgh, all you could make out was a bunch of smoky shadows all bled together. The stacks from the mills were on top, spewing out miles of black and yellow plumes.

Then came the Renaissance, and they cleaned it up a bit. Unless you were still in the thick of it, like me. Hell, we're the ones that keep the place going.

The first time my birds bred it was an accident. I'd bought a pair from the neighbor of my friend Jack, who lives in Mount Oliver. A nice yellow male and an orange female. And what do you know, the hen starts chipping away at the newspaper lining the cage and piling it up in the corner. Next thing I know she lays a couple eggs in there. Dot, I says, lookie here. That was when we had them upstairs in the living room.

I could see they wanted more privacy so I took them down to the basement and set them on my workbench. I bought a clip-on nest with some nesting material at the pet store and put those little eggs in there. In a few weeks we had our first nestling. The other didn't make it.

Starlings and pigeons will eat anything, I'm pretty sure. They hang around our lunch tables outside the mill, perching on the wires or the windowsills of the row houses across the way. And if you're not looking they'll come down and take whatever they can get. The Italians tell me they ate pigeons back in the old country. They must not be the same kinds of pigeons. Who would want to eat those oily, mangy things? They are as black as the mill.

The year my mother died I took to hunting. I was fifteen. Pap was from Germany; he told me about the wild boar they once chased right into their living room in Bavaria. Pap had an odd way of hunting, and he never quite took to it over here. I took to it myself, and it wasn't long after I learned to drive that I would skip school and go looking for deer and pheasant. Pennsylvania is chock full of them both. I killed a lot of squirrels and crows too. Seems like back then I wanted to get my hands on anything. I wanted to make sure I was freer than any other living thing, that nothing would ever get away from me again.

Pap, he remarried after a while. He got to be real quiet, and never look at you. About that time I was drafted and ended up in France. I got through Normandy but saw most everyone else blown to bits. Now that's a nightmare that only hunting and fishing can cure. I was lucky to see the war end though, and when I came back I saw Pap was quieter than ever. He barely said anything to me, just sat there smoking his pipe. So I moved out, married Dot and found a place in town. The mills were hiring and I couldn't pass it up. What else was I gonna do? Especially since Dot was already pregnant.

That kid didn't make it, but pretty soon we had another, then three more. By then we had moved back outside the city to South Hills. Pap gave us a little money to buy the lot next to his. I would never have found a better deal. So I built my house there. Pap passed away before I finished it, and my step-mom lived alone alongside us for a few years before she passed too and my sister and her family moved in.

Dot lets the neighborhood kids in to see the birds. Most of them are gone after a minute or two. But there's one who will stay down there just staring at them, one cage after another. That's Luke. He likes to ask questions too, which sometimes gets on my nerves, cause I can't always answer them. He watches me mince up the boiled eggs and vitamin mixture. I think Dot is surprised I haven't shooed him away yet. He's not like my boys—they don't give a hoot about the birds.

Now I don't mind having Luke around. It makes me think about what kind of childhood I had, and how my father treated me. Not bad, but I guess I'd say we were a little disconnected. Now Luke doesn't have a father; poor sonofabitch died a couple years ago. I remember him too—a serious but fun-loving guy. They'd come to the Christmas party. I wonder if Luke even remembers him. Dot is good friends with his mother. They live only three houses down.

I'll admit I didn't want him helping out at first. He spilled the little container of egg feed he tried to latch onto the side of the cage. And once I caught him sticking his hand in the cage of my prettiest male to try to get him to perch on his finger. Canaries don't like to do that, I said. Leave him be. Luke took a deep breath; I thought he was going to lose it. But he didn't. That's the way he is.

Of course, Luke loved Nevermore. Nevermore mostly just looked back at Luke cock-eyed, but never harmed him. Now when my beagle Sport had pups, that was another thing. I couldn't keep the little rascal away, and neither could Dot. And neither of us could convince Luke's mother to take one of them, said it was his asthma. Some doctor must have told her that, and is going to ruin the boy's childhood. I kept the puppies in a big cage I built inside my garage, and Luke would go in there and play with them. But I noticed he changed the newspaper before he left.

By and by I wondered if Luke wanted a bird to take home. Now the canaries were worth something, and I seen that he wanted a bird that would play with him. So we got Dot's sister to give up her parakeet—a pretty sky blue thing that she really didn't want anyway because it had been a gift. Luke took it home and ten minutes later the phone rings. Guess who? I let Dot handle it, and damn if the bird isn't still over there. Luckily, it's taken a liking to Luke. I told Luke he should call him that, *Lucky*. And that's what he did.

Birds can get the flu, pretty bad too, so they die. Once it starts it's hard to control. I've lost half my flock already that way. It's enough to tear you down. But the strong ones always make it through, no matter what gets thrown at them.

My arthritis is kicking up and making it harder for me to tend to them, so it might be time to let the birds go soon. If I can't sell them right away I might give 'em away, and keep one or two for ourselves. In a few more years I'll retire, and spend the day sitting on my back porch, watching the sky for whatever happens to fly by. Maybe Nevermore will come back.

Luke, he doesn't come around as often as he used to. According to his mother he's taught Lucky all sorts of tricks. That bird'll get in and out of the cage by itself, fly around the house, and land on Luke's finger. Luke was passing by on the way to the store the other day and told me all about it, how the bird knows him so well he doesn't ever mind being in a cage, knowing that when Luke comes by he'll let him out to fly around.

Caretaker

I fly in my sleep, and it's sleep I always look forward to. If it's a bad dream, I fly away from it. And if my day is just as bad, I fly away from that too. I fly away from my wife, from this city, from the life I know I will one day leave.

Some people think I raise the dead, but I don't. I raise the grass where they sleep. And in the early morning and evening, when I'm not at the cemetery, I raise pigeons.

It's the pigeons who taught me to fly.

My feet touch the ground more than others' do: I am always walking on earth, inspecting it, changing it, taking care of it. I am there under sun and in the rain. I walk it after a snowfall; I rake its leaves. All to keep the dead happy, the dead who have already flown away.

It's not a high-paying job, but it was always good enough for me. The cemetery sits on a wide hill that bends with the road alongside it, a city road with clanging streetcars, shining cars, and school kids on their bikes on the sidewalk. I can see them, but they seldom look up at me, or know I'm there. My work is quiet.

I think I've memorized just about all the stones. There are 535 of them, beginning with the ones from 1880 and moving on, at different parts of the cemetery, through the 1960s, today. I have no preference for the different styles; I only care about the grass and plants between them, and how easy or hard it is for me to tame them.

31

Some of my friends and relatives are buried here. I am always looking out for them. Hopefully they are returning the favor. Sometimes I see them in my dreams, when I'm flying. But they never speak to me.

My pigeons are Rock Pigeons. They are originally from Europe, just like my ancestors. The best ones are silvery gray, with a purplish throat and black bars on the wings. But I like seeing what variants pop up in my nests—brown and white, mottled, nearly black. It's almost as if they are adapting to every corner of this city. They all turn to face me in the morning when I approach the cages. Then I open the doors and they flap out to fill the sky. I see the silhouette of the city's skyscrapers, and the orange light coming in from the east, as they disappear over South Side. I leave the doors open, and by evening they are back in their cages, safe and ready for the next dawn.

It's funny about dying. I mean, no one seems to know much about it, but they concoct a lot of rituals and fancy agreements about how to say good-bye. I'm there at the grave site when it's all over, when the dirt has to be filled in or a headstone straightened or the mud raked after a storm. Then I see who comes back to visit—sometimes weekly, sometimes once or twice a year, sometimes never. The pact becomes very thin. I'm the only one who keeps it.

I've made friends with Father Meyer, the priest who officiates at gravesite here. He is a calm and even man. If he were an actor I'd say he was one of the best. From a distance I watch him reading the prayers and blessing the casket, always the same, never missing a beat.

Afterwards, in private, we sometimes talk. He tells me about the families that have brought him here, what might stand out. He tells me all about their lives, how long he's known them, how they have or haven't trusted him. Then he seems more like a reporter, like the guy in the gray suit on the evening news. So many expressions pass through Father Meyer's face when he's telling me about the families, but none of them ever relieves the look of worry behind his lighted blue eyes.

I don't dig the graves, but I approach them after I see the mound of fresh dirt rising among my green lanes. I make sure there are no rocks around for the faithful to step on. If they have covered any nearby bushes or flowers, I try to unearth them. People want to see that the site was prepared with care.

One morning, after the gravesite ritual, I asked Father Meyer if he ever felt useless here on this earth. If he ever felt he wasn't making a difference in the lives of the people he served. The worried look in his eyes left for a moment, then came back stronger:

"I know the work I am doing, that's all."

I had no response, so he continued:

"I believe I am helping the living to make some sense of what has happened when they lose someone. The rituals we perform together give them time, and dignity, in coming to terms with it."

"And what about the dead?"

"The dead go on in their own way. Who's to say if what we do matters to them?"

I wanted to say, *But I take care of the dead.* Instead, I said nothing. The wind blew through our ears and the tall grasses that needed mowing, leaving the gravestones untouched. Father Meyer made his way back to his car, following the mourners whose hands he had just shaken.

I went for the shed to retrieve my mower. While trimming the grass I thought of all the souls that had been deposited here: did they still roam this quiet garden? Or had they fled to other worlds, ones that did not require our tending? For whom did I tend this cemetery? For the living, or the dead?

It happens every now and again: weeks may go by without any new graves. And if it happens at certain times of the year, as it did this February, I can take a little break. This time I worked on the cages.

Some needed new wiring; others new flap doors. The birds are not easy on them. Luckily a warm spell hit. Some of the forsythia even took to blooming. I worked fast and furiously, stacking up mended coops and parceling them out to mated pairs. After I'd finished I watched the birds fly in at night. They seemed content. I watched them for a week or so before the storm hit. It was a storm that contained all the seasons, a battle among them: rain, sleet, hail, snow, and howling wind. When it was over I looked out and saw my work smashed to pieces by a fallen locust tree. None of the birds were around.

I waited a full day. But they did not come back.

A bitter cold descended on us, too cold for me to clean up the mess. The broken coops, tree limbs, and ice almost looked like a sculpture out there in the bleak yard.

Still no funerals. Nothing to do. So I took a brisk walk up Eighteenth Street to survey any damage on my grounds. To my surprise, I found Father Meyer's car parked at the entrance.

The day was warming, and I noticed puddles at my feet where they cracked through the ice. The brown and barely green grasses of my lawns were outlined blade by blade in a hoary frost. I let myself in the gate, and saw Father standing in a far corner of the cemetery, an undesirable place of few graves—those reserved for people of little means. It wasn't until I had come over the hill that I noticed the mound of dirt.

"Hello, Father. Who's this?"

"This is Felicity."

"How old?" (I noticed the small size of the grave.)

"Six. Buried two days ago, just before the storm."

"And I didn't know?"

"It happened quickly. There was no wake."

"Why not?"

"The Sisters took her in anonymously as a baby. They never found her family."

"I see. Two days ago," I muttered.

"I know. You're wondering why I'm here. I'll tell you then: I'm here paying my respects."

"Again," I said without thinking.

"I'm here for the dead this time," he said. And I noticed the calm in his eyes, how they overcame the creases in his forehead.

"I'll tidy it up a bit," I said. He thanked me, and left.

I took a rake and smoothed out the little mound, taking care to remove large stones and sending them into the woods behind me. I wondered if she would ever have a marker. Or maybe it didn't matter, since she had no one to come and see it.

I walked away from the grave and felt my head starting to spin. I felt the dead below my feet, the grief each one of them had brought to their families. I sank to my knees to steady myself, to anchor what I surely recognized as a sense of flying. Then a flurry of shadows came over me, breaking the light into pieces. Back at the edge of the woods, near the little mound, pigeons were landing, two and three at a time, their soft movements gathering until they nearly covered the grass at the site.

I rose to make my way home, my feet firmly grounded, and when I got there I found them returning also, seeking out the cages that had recently been destroyed.

Cars

She called my Uncle Norman because—I don't know why—I was bad or something. I wasn't listening, or I wanted something pretty bad and kept asking about it. And my mother, sometimes she just cries and yells. So she called him and he came and picked me up in his brand-new Buick LeSabre, silver with a red interior. It had push-button windows.

He used a voice I never heard him use before, sort of calm like a teacher. He wasn't mad at all, just tried explaining why I should listen to her and some other stuff—I forget what—but it had to do with her mostly. He turned the steering wheel with one finger, right around the bend. One finger. That was because of the power steering. After a long drive he brought me back and I went up to my room. In a while she called me down for dinner.

We have a crummy Mercury Comet, aqua-colored. The windows in back don't even go all the way down. And it's a stick-shift, so my mother is always pressing down the clutch. She uses her right hand to shift the gears from a long, bent stick coming out of the steering wheel. Once she went through a red light and a policeman pulled us over and made her cry. I didn't like that and asked him why he did that to her. He didn't answer.

I have another uncle, Uncle Jim. He's old and comes from another country, like Italy, and he has a Mercury, a nice blue color, with four doors. The neat thing about it is that the back window goes down—right behind the back seat! I think the last time I saw him was for my First Communion.

Around September the new cars start coming out, and the best place to find them—unless you go to the showroom—is Brownsville Road. Jeff and I go down there on Saturdays to sit on the corner and watch out for them.

I make a checklist with all the Chevys, Pontiacs, Buicks, Dodges, Chryslers, Fords, and Cadillacs I can think of. As soon as we see a new model we check it off the list. The corner is good because they have to stop there at the light and we can get a good look at them. The best year was 1967, because that's the year every new car had side-signals: little red rectangles on the sides of the bumpers that light up when you used a turn signal.

Another way to find the new cars is to look through magazines. The ads start before the new models are on the road, so we have some time to memorize them and get excited about seeing them. They always look so nice in those magazines, and they travel in neat places with palm trees or cactuses. New cars can take you anywhere.

Then there is the Five-and-Ten. They have lots of models to buy, and little jars of paint in every color you can think of to paint them with. You can buy, say, a 1964 Mustang and paint it any color you want—even one of the metallic ones that glitter. Some of the little pieces are hard to glue, but you can always paint over the rough spots.

I have a set of encyclopedias in my room. The spine on each book is a different color, and together they make a rainbow. One of my dad's cousin's sold them to us. They still smell new, kind of like Elmers glue but sweeter. I like to look through them. I'll just pick a color and pull down the book and start paging through it. I especially like the articles about different countries, and sometimes I just go from one country to another. They might have palm trees.

My favorite part is the little box that has words from the language they speak in that country. It tells you how to pronounce them too. I read them out loud, over and over, until I think it sounds natural. Then I really think I'm in Italy, or France, or maybe Japan.

The only way I get around my neighborhood, besides walking, is with my red bike. There are a lot of hills here, but I'm used to them. To go up a hill you just go criss-cross, and slow, so your legs don't go numb. If you're lucky, after climbing a long hill you'll get to go down one. Then you can let go of the handlebars and sail like a bird, with the wind brushing your ears.

If Jeff and I go far down our street we're in for some surprises, because we won't know for sure what kind of hills we'll have to pedal up, or where all the side streets will take us. It's easy to get lost. Then we have to find our way back home. But it can be fun getting lost, like being in a different country. Except no palm trees.

Jeff went on a vacation once. He was gone for a whole week. I read a lot of encyclopedias that week, and didn't ride my bike once.

Jeff and his family went to someplace called Ocean City. They had to drive *eight hours* to get there. Jeff has a Chevy station wagon, so they can fit him and his brothers and sister in there and put their suitcases on top in a special box. I watched them pull away. Jeff's dad was driving with sunglasses on. He waved to me.

When they came back Jeff was very dark. He closed his arm up to make the skin inside his elbow even darker. I compared it to mine, but even though I went swimming about every day in the summer his was still darker. I asked him what it was like there. Was the ocean scary? Could you really float on it? Did he see any neat cars?

Plenty, he said. They passed by so many new cars on the highway he could hardly keep track of them. They were form all over, too: New Jersey, New York, Maryland, Virginia. Even Illinois! Were they all going to the ocean? I think so, he said; where else could they be going? Were they all full of families? Of course they were!

I decided we hadn't gone far enough on our bikes, so I asked my mother if I could ride with Jeff down to my grandparents' house, which was pretty far down Brownsville Road, past three cemeteries and two car showrooms. What if you're tired when you get there, she said. Then you can come and get us, or grandpap can drive us home. Oh well, okay then, but be careful and call me when you get there.

We could have ice cream on the way.

Lucky we picked a nice day for our trip, but it was hot. Our first stop was Isaly's, at the corner where we sit and watch for cars. I got a chocolate ice cream with marshmallow topping. Jeff got hot fudge on vanilla. Then we started down Brownsville. After every turn we found something I never saw when passing by in our Comet. It was like time slowing down. We saw lots of other boys riding their bikes or horsing around, boys we'd never seen before. It was almost like being in another country, because now we were in Carrick, and it sure felt different. The houses were big and old, with giant front porches and attics. Some had boxes with geraniums planted in them. I like the way geranium leaves smell, like my grandparents' cellar, but fresher. We always plant geraniums on my father's grave, and we passed that too. If the cemetery didn't have such a long hill to go down we might have gone to visit him.

The Chevy showroom came after another cemetery, and by now we were in Mt. Oliver. We slowed to look inside but we'd already seen those models because it was summer and they'd already been out for almost a year.

Just before my grandparents' street was the pizza place my mother sometimes stops at. I could smell the pizza when we passed it.

Margaret Street is also a big, long hill, and luckily we were going down it, because they live near the bottom. We rode on the sidewalk though because their road is made of bumpy old brick. We passed Raciopi's, the little store half-way down that sells penny candy.

Nana was surprised to see us. I don't think my mother told her we were coming. So the first thing she did was call her. Then she gave us root beer and sandwiches, even though it was only three o'clock.

Grandpap wasn't home. He was up at the top of Margaret Street in his bar. I've been in that bar. They have a little duckpin alley and Grandpap lets me play it. I asked Nana if she wanted us to go and get him, but she said no, he would be home soon.

Just then he walked in. He gave me a kiss with his scratchy beard and shook hands with Jeff. I could smell the beer on him. Then he went to pee. When he came back he said he needed some help in the garden, so we went out the back door and down the steps to the yard.

Next door, on the other side of the hedges, I could see the Stambroskis' grapes growing. Mrs. Stambroski always spoke another language with my grandmother. It wasn't Polish. Nana said they could understand each other anyway.

Jeff and I pulled a bunch of weeds out from around the corn and cucumber plants while my grandfather watched and poked the ground with his cane. After a while I got pretty tired and so did Jeff. Nana came out with some water for us. She said my mother would be driving down to get us and we'd try to stuff the bikes into the back seat and trunk of the car somehow. We could all sit in the front then.

I knew it would take a while for her to get there, so me and Jeff went for a little walk in the alley that ran behind my grandparent's house, behind a tall row of hedges and a little gate my grandfather put there. Once we were through that gate we saw a hillside of woods, and a couple of old houses along the alley. We followed it to the very end, and it came out at the bottom of Margaret Street, across from Verscharen's greenhouse. That's where we bought the geraniums.

The greenhouse was open, so we walked through it. It went on forever, each glass room full of a different kind of flower. It smelled all warm and comfortable in there, but we had to leave. Mr. Verscharen said goodbye to us. He's from Germany.

On the way home I fell asleep leaning against my mother. I could hear the buzzing under the wheels when we drove over brick roads, then stop when we reached pavement. My ears were turning on and off, and the wind that came in through the windows blew around my face.

Raquel and I

In sixth grade my skin changed. It seems funny but I'm sure it happened: it became more oily, shiny, even on my arms. It smelled different. My hair changed too. It's darker now, and I comb it. But there's that picture of me from that year—my school picture—that makes me look in-between. Maybe my whole life will revolve around that year.

Now I'm much older—thirteen—and every day when I wake up I feel like I've never lived before, like there will be some surprise that day. Usually there is.

Yesterday it was Lynn Gruber. Today it's Dani Hrasko. Lynn's blonde and Dani's a brunette. Her hair falls straight, parted down the middle just like Marlo Thomas on *That Girl*. From history class I can see her across the hall, sitting with her legs pressed together under that short skirt. She smells nice. I think Sister Venard sees me looking at her. I feel a little lost, like I did that day when my group had to get up to give our presentation and I had a hard-on.

I keep faces in my desk drawer, the old beat-up desk that was my father's, in the corner cubby of our bedroom. My brothers don't go in there much. That's where I study, and paint, and think a lot. It has a little window.

In the drawer I have Elizabeth Taylor (who just turned 40, it says), Carly Simon, Marilyn Monroe, Rita Hayworth (she was a pinup from

World War Two) and Greta Garbo. I like to study their faces. Each one is so different, but I can't help looking at them over and over. Especially Greta Garbo.

Last month, after art school, I came home and painted Carly Simon. I used a thick brush for a small canvas, and I painted oranges and reds in thick strokes for the background.

I go to the same art school my uncle went to on Saturday mornings. I have my favorites there too. After the lecture, when we go off to draw or paint in the museum, I notice the same girls week after week, their faces that make me think of Vermeers or Raphaels or even El Grecos, and their bodies that are so different from mine. I like the way they pull their hair to one side, or the way they look when they are concentrating on their drawings. I do quick sketches of them on the back of my drawing pad.

At school they always ask me to decorate the bulletin boards. I've been doing it since fourth grade, and I used to like it. Now I just think it's weird.

Valentine's Day is what got me into trouble.

I could have cut out a bunch of pink and red hearts, which aside from being embarrassing would have been just plain boring. So I drew some figures—women holding champagne glasses—to pin to the ends of the long board, and then I put the "Happy Valentines Day" going big across the middle. Now our principal Sister Margaret gave the board a quick glance when she came in for a short visit, but said nothing. The next day, when she popped in again and saw the poster of Raquel Welch wearing her *One Million Years B. C.* fur bikini on the tall side board, she turned to stone. "Who put that up there?" she demanded. I raised my hand. "See me down in my office."

Now Sister Margaret looked like a business woman in her conservative, knee-length suits and very short hair. She ran the school like a business, and even tried to do some nice things for us from time to time. She arranged for a woman from Gimbel's make-up department to come and teach the seventh and eighth grade girls how to apply it. Even Judith Zagorski looked better, I have to admit.

Sister had never had a problem with me, one of the school's star pupils. I wasn't even sure what I had done wrong. They did ask me to decorate the bulletin boards, right? So I brought in one of my favorite posters just to fill the space until I could think of something else to put up there. As I was leaving the room to head down to her office my homeroom teacher, Mister Kelly, said, "I'm sorry Luke. We should have said something earlier." "That's okay," I replied, not knowing what I was in for.

I passed Sister Margaret in the hall downstairs just before I reached her office. "I'll be in shortly," she said, and went off to attend to some other business which obviously had superceded mine.

So I sat in the chair in front of her desk, thinking. It was a nice day outside. Funny, I almost forgot why I was there. And then a thought sent a shiver up my spine. What if Sister Venard had told her about the day she found me kissing Clare Simicki in the supply closet? Was that why she was bearing a grudge? Just the thought of holding Clare and smelling her breath put me in a better mood.

I waited there for at least an hour. Was this a form of psychological torture? Sister's office was so neat and calm. Everything was in order there but me. But by the time she did come in I was starting to feel very peaceful and relaxed.

She pulled up the chair behind her desk and sat down, at first not looking at me.

"Do you know why you are here?"

"Because of the poster?" I ventured. "I bought it at the art store."

"The art store?"

"At Carnegie-Mellon, where I go to art school."

She took a deep breath.

"Do you think it's appropriate?"

"I was getting tired of doing the bulletin boards."

"Mister Kelly and Sister Venard say you do a very good job with the boards."

"Do they? Thank you."

"About the poster. We don't portray women that way in this school."

"Sorry."

"Is there anything else you'd like to say about it?"

"No. Well, just that I was bored with doing the bulletin boards and I had this poster I liked, so I brought it in—"

"I see. And you didn't think it might offend anyone?"

"No. I mean, I guess not. It's a nice poster. But, I don't know. Maybe."

"I'd like you to think about this and come back tomorrow to tell me why you think it might be wrong."

"Okay."

She stood up as I was leaving, and I expected her to say something else, but she didn't.

Back in the classroom I noticed Mister Kelly had already taken the poster down and rolled it up for me to take home. We continued on with math class, and no one spoke to me for the rest of the day.

I walked home thinking about Sister's request: why it was wrong to hang up a picture of a beautiful woman. I couldn't come up with anything, so I asked my sister about it. She was in tenth grade at the high school.

"What? Are you crazy? You took that poster to school?"

That was all she said, so I still didn't have a clue.

At dinnertime my mother spoke up: "Sister Margaret called me today. She told me about the poster."

"Oh?" I could feel myself turning red.

"I don't know what this poster is, but she seemed very upset about it."

"It's a poster of Raquel Welch wearing a fur bikini."

My sister let out a little burst of laughter, which she tried to hide behind a smile.

"Why don't you think of something else to hang up tomorrow?" my mother said.

"Okay. I don't know what though."

"You'll think of something."

I finished my dinner quickly and went to my cubby.

It wasn't that Raquel Welch was my favorite; I just didn't have anything as big and captivating as that poster to put up. I thought the black-and-white was nice too. Anything but those construction paper colors I'd been using for eight years! I started thinking about Valentine's Day, and love, and what they meant. I was lost; I didn't know. I only knew what I liked, and what I felt.

I thought of all the things I had loved: chocolate licorice, tropical fish, model cars, spring. How was it possible to make sense of them all together? What about my drawer full of beautiful women? I loved them too, even though a lot of them were dead. Did love have to be alive, or could it be dead? Did I love any one of them, even Greta Garbo, more than the others? More than I loved my grandparents, or my mother?

I began paging through my pile of *Life* and *National Geographic* magazines. I don't know why—I wanted to look at pictures. Pictures of anything. Anything that caught me. The first interesting thing I found was a baseball player being surrounded and hugged by his teammates. Then I saw a worried woman from some place in Asia wearing a colorful scarf, resting her chin on her hand. Next came pictures of animals: a group of lions lounging under a tree, a giant flock of penguins who all looked content, a hummingbird in mid-air drinking from a large red flower. I cut out a picture of President Nixon holding his wife's hand, and Jackie Onassis sailing on her husband's yacht. I found a farmer holding a bushel of cornstalks, and some Indians from the Amazon with holes in their ears.

I sat there until midnight cutting out anything I liked, until I had a nice stack of photos of all sizes sitting on my desk. I went to bed thinking about them, filling up with the feeling they gave me.

I slept well and awoke earlier than usual, so I decided to walk early to school, carrying my pile of photos in my bag.

The front door of the building was still locked but I saw Bernie the janitor at a side door, and he let me in. Up on the third floor, where my homeroom was, the lights were on. Sister Venard was busy in her room at her desk, and she saw me pass by.

"Do you have permission to be here?" she said.

"I'm doing the bulletin board…"

Before I could finish explaining Mister Kelly came up the steps. "It's okay, Sister."

She nodded and dropped her head back down to her work, looking like a statue in church with her black veil and white habit. She was older than Sister Margaret and hadn't yet adopted civilian dress.

I unloaded my bag and got to work. Mister Kelly had things to do as well, so he didn't bother me. I had a rough idea of how I wanted this to look, but I could only get that idea out by working, and moving the pictures around. At first I used pins to hold them in place, and when I was satisfied with the collage I had created, I stapled everything in place. The board was completely covered, except in the center where I had left a small empty space where the cork showed through. I cut out a black square, about six inches or so, and attached it there. And onto the black box, filling it to size, I pasted a white heart. By that time the classroom was filling up with kids.

Valentine's Day came the next morning, and though I'd bought them, I decided not to bring in my goofy little kids' cards for everyone. I decided the joke wasn't that funny. I did notice everyone staring at my newly decorated bulletin board, studying the photos intently, as they had the day before. I even caught Mister Kelly poring over them after he'd handed out the algebra quiz, and asking me where I'd found some of them. Sister Margaret wasn't around. I heard her mother had died in Columbus during the night. We had to pray for her.

The snowstorm hit later in the week, and school was cancelled for two days, which brought us to the weekend. Then, strangely, it became very warm, and there were steamy puddles everywhere.

Back at school on Monday the first thing we heard on the announcements was Mrs. DeLucia's voice. She was our school secretary, and she said that Sister Margaret would be away for another week or two. She didn't say why, but that we should still pray for her. I wondered how to pray for something when you don't know what you're praying for.

The end of February came, and I dreaded coming up with something to put up for March. I thought of tacking up a real bird's nest, but didn't think I could find one that had survived the winter. Maybe some large stripes of color, an abstract expressionist bulletin board? I was undecided. But I had to take down February, so I came in early again, had a few words with Sister Venard, and looked around in Mister Kelly's desk drawer for the staple remover. When I turned around, there was Sister Margaret, looking very, very tired, but somehow very strong underneath.

"Morning Sister."

"Hello Luke."

"Sorry to hear about your mother."

"Thank you."

"I was just taking down this board."

She turned toward it.

"Yes. I saw it last night. We had a PTO meeting in here. Many of the parents commented on it."

"Good or bad?"

"Good, of course! You did a nice job."

"Thanks."

"It really shows—" she stopped.

"Shows what?"

"I don't know."

"Love. It's love. For Valentine's Day."

"I guess that's it."

"I wanted to show it all around. All different kinds of it."

She nodded, not looking at me, but the board.

I began removing the pictures, and as I took care to remove the staples from them she helped gather the photos into a neat pile, stuydying each one carefully, as if they were something more delicate, more permanent than one month's display. Then she looked up at the clock and left.

I took the pictures home after school and put them in another drawer of my father's old desk. I never looked at them again.

Brothers

There was a time, I guess, when I saw the beauty in winter, the fields filling softly with down, the sky erased by descending shades of white-speckled gray. There was the silence too, the hush that I thought was in my soul. Now I only see the shoveling at dawn, followed by sliding wheels and a filmy windshield as I try to make it to Pitt's campus on time.

Not that I don't like teaching. After I get there, having collected my thoughts during the drive, I begin rehearsing my hand gestures and pauses. These are the details that make my students remember the message. With philosophy, the delivery is all too important, proving the relativity of words in the way they are presented and therefore understood. I suppose I first learned that in the monastery.

The hard part is, I'm not only lecturing, I'm looking at their faces too. Beautiful faces, full of discovery, faces soaking in everything I say until my words dance like lights in their eyes. I feel I'm falling in love with every one of them. And if I fall in love over and over again, does it diminish love or enlarge it? A philosophical question, I know. But that's what I do.

Lately I've been dating someone named Carol. She's not a student, so I can't be called a patronizing professor, even if I'm not quite thirty. I met her at the mimeograph machine. She works for the dean.

I can't say what it is about her exactly, but I enjoy her company. She has a sweet face, adorable blue eyes, and a way of crinkling up her nose when she disapproves of something. When she looks at me, she never looks away like some people do. I find it interesting that she put herself through college. We never have trouble finding something to talk about.

When I first left the monastery I found girls fascinating. Not because I was sex-starved exactly, but because, well, they were so *different.* I noticed the way they smelled, how they laughed, the stupid things they talked about. It was refreshing after having lived for two years with a lot of stale-smelling men in brown tunics who were not allowed to speak.

I didn't have trouble with the silence. At first I welcomed it, and hearing the beautiful chants five times a day made me think that the human voice was best employed by singing. But silence encourages thought, and thought encourages perception. I began to see things in a new way, some for the first time. And often those perceptions kept me up at night, intruding on my prayers.

Among us was a bright-hearted boy, Peter McGrath. Where most of us battled our inner demons daily, begging God's mercy on our conflicted souls, Peter McGrath seemed to be cut from the heavens, so at peace with himself that it was comforting to be working beside him. His wide brown eyes reminded you of a favorite pet; his fine lips betrayed no ill feelings, but hinted always of a genuine smile.

Where was Brother McGrath from? We didn't know, as these things were deemed unimportant in the monastery. How old was he? It was difficult to say—early twenties, maybe even thirty? We never saw his family visit, yet he never showed feelings of loneliness or abandonment. Peter was the model novice, and we were certain that one day he would be leading the monastery.

Gethsemani was in Kentucky, on the fringe of the Appalachians. Before entering I had never thought of myself as much of a nature buff. But once there, and thoroughly adapted to the natural rhythms of wakefulness in daylight and sleep at sundown, I began to appreciate the habits of birds and other wildlife. We seemed to be related in a greater way than I had previously imagined.

During the afternoon, my chores done and midday prayers recited, I had some time for contemplation. Often I'd take one of our paths through the woods, which led to wooden or stone benches here and there, along with contemporary sculptures of the Virgin, Jesus, and the Buddha. On my favorite days, I'd sit there among the trees and feel the sunlight stroking me intermittently between clouds. Or, during winter, I'd marvel at the crystalline snow and the bared souls of trees. I found solace there at any time of year.

Peter McGrath often made his way there too, and at times we'd spy each other, nod cheerfully, then retreat to our singular contemplative worlds. But in a way it was comforting to know he was near.

The vow of silence was not hard to bear, because as I said it did serve to bring new things to light. What we didn't speak was revealed in other ways, whether willed or not.

It didn't take long for us to notice that Brother McGrath had left. This was not really strange. The life of a monk is not for everyone, and novices disappeared regularly and at random. What was strange was that another novice, brother Raymond Lunghi, had vanished also. Brother Lunghi was the troubled one, quite the opposite of Brother McGrath and his cheerful eyes. Brother Lunghi was not as mysterious. We knew he had come from New York, that he was the third of five brothers, and that his father had died just prior to his entrance to Gethsemani. But, whereas the rest of us had come to Gethsemani to find contemplation and prayer, willing to make the sacrifices necessary for that kind of life, one got the feeling that Brother Lunghi had come as a refugee, an escapist of sorts. He seldom made eye contact—one of the necessary ways we communicated.

Shortly after the departure of Brothers McGrath and Lunghi I found myself sitting on my favorite bench on the woodland path. I had lost myself completely when Brother Sokol approached, so quietly that at first I'd thought it was nothing but the rustling of a small bird.

"Brother Lashide," he said, "I would like to speak with you about something."

After a moment or two I replied: "If something is troubling you, perhaps you should visit your confessor."

"Something is very troubling, but I doubt that our confessor will be able to console me."

"What is it?"

"It's about Brother McGrath."

I lost another moment, then responded: "Brother McGrath is gone."

"I know why he left."

"He couldn't commit?"

"No, that wasn't it. He and Brother Lunghi—both of them—they were having relations."

I retreated into silence again, for I knew that was the best way to accept what I'd just heard. Brother Sokol looked confused though, and I couldn't bear to see him suffering, so I spoke:

"We are told that's a grave sin."

"We are. But—Brother McGrath. *Brother McGrath!*"

I felt the world rush out of me, the world I so loved. In its place entered terror.

"Why?" I said.

"That is what troubles me, Brother Lashide. Why devour the good with the senseless?"

"I don't know," I said. "I don't know the answer to that. Maybe it lies in prayer."

"Or maybe it lies beyond this monastery."

We hadn't noticed, but Father Becker was walking along the path toward us. He passed by, holding his hand to his lips. We obliged.

I fell asleep that evening after compline and didn't awaken for midnight prayer. I had been thinking about Brother McGrath, about how he was able to communicate so much without using our habitual, tarnished words. It was a gift. I wondered if it was love.

In the following days I became distracted, unable to keep pace with the monastic rhythm, which I had prided myself in mastering. I missed the source of strength that Brother McGrath had given us. The monastery, whether inside the chapel, in the bread kitchen, or walking the trails, seemed a darker place. I could no longer feel protected there. My worries, much as I tried to overcome them with prayer, increased.

I began to feel so distant from the brotherhood that my eyes betrayed it. I began to attract long glances from some of the brothers. My chants were lifeless. The woods could not console me.

Finally, after ten days of this heart-breaking, aimless wandering, I decided to leave the monastery. I have never been back.

I am used to the secular world again. And though it is troubling, I am even more fascinated by it than I had been as a child. I see folly everywhere, but I find an equal amount of effort and good faith reflected in the lives of those I meet.

About love, I don't know. My time in the monastery was spent contemplating love—the love that comes from divine inspiration. But what about the human kind? Love was everywhere I looked, even when it was disguised as competition, brutality, or coyness. Love was unbearable, and yet it kept me afloat.

My students often come to visit me as I sit in my office ruminating on coming lectures. At first they may be shy or even suspicious of my position. But invariably I put them at ease, and we talk about anything that digresses from philosophy. Philosophy is life, I tell them. That's why we must take it seriously. They challenge me without realizing that that is what I most prize, and consider a vindication of my teaching methods. And just before they leave I almost always see it: that glint of Peter McGrath in their eyes.

I remember now those quiet hours Brother McGrath and I spent in the woods on our benches, the gentle glances he occasionally threw my way which I never returned. We would pass each other in the halls of the monastery, quietly as usual, and I felt as if he were reaching out to me in some way, as I've said, without words.

Maybe Brother McGrath knew the secret of love, the constant expression of love—both the divine and the human kinds. Maybe for him they were one and the same. Maybe the lessons we all learned at Gethsemani were nothing next to the blood-and-bone lesson of our unspoken Brother McGrath.

The Magnolia Branch

It happened one April night when the magnolia tree was blooming. The tree was pink and white, lighted by the moon and a streetlamp. It grew in front of an old stone house halfway between the universities, across the street from another stone house, which was labeled, *Historic Landmark*. Inside both homes husbands snored their wives to sleep.

It had been six months since the two of them had met. Neither of them could remember the actual day or time of the meeting, or even where they had been or why they had been together.

He simply called her now, safe in his private room down the hall from his loud roommates, six months from the last time he had seen her. As he dialed her number he thought of how she would respond: "You wouldn't believe the work they give you at this school. You should come up and see my work sometime. Tonight? I just can't— well, I don't know. I just can't."

"Hello?"

"Jean? It's me."

"Luke!" Her voice lightened. "How are you, Mister Sarda?"

"Great. Hey, you busy tonight? There's a party over at the House."

"Luke, you should see what I have to do here."

"What are you doing?"

"Now? Drawing. I just figured I'd stay up and draw tonight."

"Come on. I'll be over in a half-hour."

She paused; he had already decided she wouldn't go.

"Okay."

"Good. See you then."

He hadn't seen her in six months, maybe longer, since before Christmas. It always happened like this, though; always when they'd least expect it. One of them would call and it would be as if they spoke to each other every day. He wondered how she kept her hair now, now that she had transferred to the architecture school at the other university. He knew they dressed differently there; he had known she would fit right in.

He felt a little anxious but knew he shouldn't, because he knew that once they met their anxiety would be gone. It always happened this way.

He remembered one of their meetings, one when they had been in high school, when they lived at opposite ends of the city and saw each other twice a year. He remembered the time he walked up the steps leading to the front porch of her house. It must have been summer, though he couldn't remember what month. It might have been August, because the leaves were all lost in steam around the convent across from her house; they walked through the hillside convent grounds that evening, and felt the skin around their eyes become moist. He remembered this night well now, as he stood before the mirror in his bedroom and looked for a shirt to wear.

Their lives were lives of days. For her the days were so filled she could hardly ever keep track of engagements. He knew this, because he felt he was sometimes the same way. For the six or seven times she would forget to call him back there would be one when she would remember. On these days, the days that could only be filled by him, they would meet somewhere and spend the hours together. These days, two or three a year, accumulated in each of them so that they felt themselves living different lives those days; they felt somehow better, somehow released from their normal lives on those few days.

For all the times they called each other (he called more often than she) only a handful would result in their meeting. When such a day as today came they would be busy with their separate lives until they met. Even when they met it was not shocking. They would look at each other and decide where to go, what to do. Then, by the end of the day, after they had separated again, they would both realize how strong and peaceful it had felt, as if they had not been together at all, but only with themselves.

He looked into the mirror again and thought about the last time they had been together. He could not remember it exactly. He remembered many days they had spent together; fragments of these days came up as he thought. But dates he could not remember.

He wore a light jacket; it was actually cool that evening, but his fingertips were warm and even a little numb. He had exercised and gone to classes that day. He wasn't tired at all; he had almost filled the day. Now he realized the day was beginning all over again. He walked through the level oak-lined streets; old homes lined the streets, homes with front yards planted in evergreens and rhododendrons.

He came to the other campus after a twenty-minute walk.

She was ready as soon as he'd knocked. He couldn't believe it: her hair was loose, unstyled; she wore a large shirt with the tails out over her pants. They walked back along main streets to the house where his friends had their regular Saturday night party.

They remembered her at the party. He watched his friends' faces, their reactions to seeing her again. She was very attractive. Some of them put their arms around her and smiled; others stopped while walking past and said, "Jean!" Then they would have little to say.

It happened over and over again that night; they all loved seeing her again, and they were glad for him, because he always spoke of her and they thought he loved her.

She enjoyed laughing with them again; he stood near her and sometimes smiled. At the other parties he would be running up and down the stairs; he would be the one putting his arms around friends and laughing.

They both decided to leave after an hour. Back at his apartment she was amused by a small cat a friend had given him. She sat on the floor, leaning against the bottom of the torn couch; he decided he liked the way she kept her hair now. It just fell from her head all around, a little shaggy, but shiny, like washed nylon rope. It was light brown.

They stayed there until three o'clock, leaning against the couch while the black-and-white cat stalked their hands.

She had to be up early the next morning, seven o'clock. She said: "Luke?"

"What?"

She looked down, then up again. "Could I stay here tonight?"

Just as he was about to say yes she spoke again: "Maybe I should just go home."

"You'll never be up in time if you stay."

They both knew it wouldn't really matter, because there would be other days like this one. When they were able to be together it seemed as though they met every day, so they never felt the need to take advantage of time.

"Come see my room," he said.

It was a closet-sized room behind the kitchen.

"Luke! It's so small!"

"I know, but I like it."

"I do too."

She was a little taller than he and he was glad she wouldn't spend the night, because it would have been embarrassing in that small room. The cat walked in and they felt suddenly crowded. He picked up their jackets and they left.

It was a slow walk. All the parties along the main road were finished now. A few lights shone on the third floors of the buildings. It was April, and still very cool in the middle of the night. Twice a car passed them and they listened to it drone further down the road. She said it was actually cold out; he helped her wrap a scarf around her neck. She held her hands deep in her jacket pockets and looked at him with her nose covered by the scarf. Then she slipped her hand through his arm, and held it close.

They turned a corner onto a smaller road; professors and other professionals lived on this road. There was hardly any wind. The moon was out but they didn't look up at it; its light combined with light from the streetlamps. The road curved and both saw splotches of streetlamp light dotting the sidewalk, following the curve of the road.

He stopped and she looked at him. He was looking at the magnolia tree.

"Look how bright the petals are," he said. He walked over to the tree.

"Luke!" she whispered. She thought the yard was pretty and didn't want him spoiling it. He picked a twig with a flower on its end and brought it back. The flower wasn't all opened yet. He smelled it first and gave it to her.

They began walking again and she looked at the flower in her hand. Before they came to the end of the road, where it intersected another main road, he thought of something to say:

"Jean, if we never get married, at least we know we were married tonight."

He didn't feel awkward saying this; he would never have said it during his real life, but life was different on these few days they spent together. They could say whatever came into their minds and not think about how the other would react, because it was as though they were speaking to themselves.

She had been imagining the same thing; she broke off a bud which grew at the bottom of the twig, and gave it to him.

"Here, this is your boutonniere."

He liked the idea, and put it through a button hole in his collar.

"You know," he said, "did you ever think that someday when you want to get married you'll plan it for a certain day, and that day will come, but you just might not feel like getting married that day?"

She smiled and nodded.

"That would be horrible. Why should you do something if you don't feel like it? Just think of all the things you would have to do—the church, reception, and people taking pictures—and if you didn't feel like being there that particular day, it would be awful."

"I guess I never thought about it that way," she said.

He had said too much; they walked the rest of the way in silence. When they arrived at her building they stood by the door for a while. A cat jumped out at them and went up to the door, so they let it in. She'd never seen it before. They both watched it inside the building now and laughed. Then he picked it up to carry it out again; he was ready to leave.

"Thank you, Mister Sarda," she said.

"You're welcome."

She kissed him.

"Don't forget about the show."

"What show?"

"My show—the class, I mean."

"Oh, okay."

He knew he would never see it; they always made plans like this. They made twenty plans and only one would be followed through. He kissed her again and left with the cat.

Outside he let the cat go and walked home the same route they had walked. He passed the magnolia tree again and stopped to watch its pink-and-white brightness before going on.

At his apartment he took a whiskey glass and filled it partway with water; then he set the magnolia bud into it, and put it on his dresser in his small bedroom.

The next morning the bud had opened fully; he looked at it but could not remember exactly what it had meant. He would try calling her again in a few weeks.

He never got in touch with her during the summer. In the fall he transferred to another school, outside the state. One day he opened his mailbox and found a letter from her. He read the letter and found that she was getting married to someone he had never heard her speak of before. He went back to his room to sit and think a while. Then he wrote her back to wish her good luck; he wrote as if they spoke to each other every day, and he dropped the letter into the mailbox on his way to class.

Bloomfield

We got this apartment after looking around almost the whole city. I wanted to live in Sou'side, I guess because I grew up there and everyone's Polish. Not that I don't like Italians—I married one. Bloomfield's almost all Italian. We can see Pittsburgh from here, or really just the Gulf building sticking up behind Saint Stanislaus on Polish Hill. On clear days the sunsets over the city are marvelous—reds, oranges, violet. We're up on a hill but it levels out on top so it's easy to get around. You can take Bigelow Boulevard from town, go across the bridge and get here in about five minutes, depending on traffic. Or you can come up Liberty Avenue. Liberty's nice; it rises out of the city and brings you straight into the business center of Bloomfield. Besides Italians, there are some Poles and Germans here; there's Mierzwa's pharmacy and Bauer's bakery. Mum takes a streetcar here from Mount Oliver through Sou'side and town before reaching Bloomfield. Mum brings groceries. She would come on Saturdays before I quit work; now she comes any time. And she brings her damn dust rag.

The first time I saw my place I wanted to cry. The walls were yellow (used to be white), closets weren't big enough to hold a pair of shoes, and the worst thing—I saw a roach in the kitchen sink. Sam talked me into it though; it was about all we could afford. Well I've cleaned up messes before and I cleaned up this one. Sam painted the walls one weekend before studying all night. I washed the floors with Lysol and scrubbed every inch of that sink; I'll be damned if I ever want to see another roach. It's only two rooms so we didn't have to get much furniture. I found a beautiful set of aqua nylon living room chairs and couch. Mum bought us a beige rug. I didn't want to accept it at first but Sam talked me into it again; told me not to be so stubborn. He's always right. We have a black metal lamp standing between the two chairs. We don't have a T.V. I'm throwing hints at Sam for one now that I'm home all day with nothing to do. Sam's mum made us sheer curtains; she doesn't even use a ruler when she puts a hem on them. Our bed folds up into a closet in the living room. I can never get it down alone and it's so heavy I'm afraid I'll hurt myself. A couple times a leg fell off and we had to screw it back on.

There was a kitchen table here already; it has an ugly gray formica top. My copper-bottomed pots are the only nice thing about my kitchen. I made Sam *gołąbki* yesterday in the dutch oven. They turned out better than mum's. The walls in my kitchen are clean white now; I hung a few potholders above the stove. There's two big windows but they stick during the summer and I can never get them open. The floor is checkered with cream and green tile—reminds me of Lenny's where I worked as a soda-jerk. My pantry has pretty wooden doors. I keep all my canned food, rice, coffee, spaghetti (I can make good sauce now), and dishes there; it's right outside of the kitchen at the top of the stairs. Sam's poor mother has to climb three flights when she comes to see us. I usually help her on the way down; the banister's broken in some parts. On Saturdays we go shopping—sometimes the three of us— mum, Sam's mum, and me.

Sam's mum always wants to stop at the *Groceria Italiana*. The Groceria's off of Liberty a half block. It's a small place; all the Italian women shop there on Saturday afternoons. It's only a ten minute walk from my place on Pacific Avenue—through the square, past Saint Francis' Hospital and the Church of the Immaculate Conception. The first time I walked into the Groceria I thought I'd throw up. All you can smell is that cheese they put on their spaghetti, reminds me of stinking feet. Sam's mum buys that cheese and home-made noodles; I stand in the aisle and bite my lip. My mum, with a poke through her arm and a babushka on, helps Sam's mum with her bags. Mister D'Amico at the register always asks me if I want some pickles or something—just to make us laugh.

From the Groceria we move onto Liberty. There are always old Italian men sitting on steps or standing around the street corner smoking cigars. Sam's mum stops and talks to them; they grab me by the cheek and wink at me. But it sounds so nice to hear them talk. Across the street Saint Joseph's and its rectory take up half a block. Maggio's is to the left of it, where I get pizza for dinner sometimes. Then there's Bloomfield's Men's Store, where I bought Sam these underwear with red hearts on them. The bad thing about Liberty Avenue is there's no trees on it. They cut them down because they were getting into the telephone and electric wires. So now there's this four lane road with stores back to back all the way down both sides and no trees.

Two blocks down from Saint Joseph's on the right is Kroger's. It's right across from the Bloomfield Bridge. We go there to do most of our food shopping. They have a good produce section, at least six different kinds of lettuce. Italians are always having salads with their meals. Up from Kroger's is Lenny's, where Sam has his internship for pharmacy school. It's not a very big drugstore but it has a soda fountain. Del's is across the street from Lenny's on the same side as the bridge. Sam and I ate there last Friday night; I had lasagna and Sam had some kind of Italian dumplings with sauce. His mother makes them better. There are a few antique shops by Del's. Sometimes we look around in them to see if there's anything for the apartment. My mum and Sam's mum can't understand why anyone would want to buy old cruddy things for a house. I don't mind shopping with them most of the time but at times I'd rather go alone.

When I'm by myself I walk all the way down Liberty to Shadyside. Usually I stop at Isaly's for a sundae on the way. One of these days I'll have the money to buy something from Shadyside—maybe one of those paintings from the art stores or a hat from those expensive clothes stores. Shadyside's a little more spread out than Bloomfield; the people aren't as friendly there.

On the way back I walk up Liberty and turn down South Millvale Street right past the hospital. Behind the hospital I come out at the square. A lot of women like to sit on the benches in the square and talk. It's as big as a football field, maybe two. Not really a lot of trees there, but it's covered with grass. Friendship Avenue circles the square and there are cars on it all the time, but nobody seems to mind. Kids play there every day after school. Maria, my neighbor, already has four; she's there on Saturdays with her youngest, Angela, in a stroller. The nurses from Saint Francis are out there on their lunch hour; Sam's first cousin Gloria works there too and she's out sometimes.

I used to go straight home after the square, but I've really gotten into the habit of walking more lately. It's supposed to be good for me anyway. On hot days I walk over to Sam's mother's or to his Aunt Mary's. Sam's mother lives at the other end of South Pacific, that is, on the other side of the square from us. The square cuts three other roads in two: Atlantic, Melville, and Mathilda. They're all lined with sugar maples; Sam's Aunt Mary lives on Mathilda.

Aunt Mary's always sitting on the front porch of her red brick house fanning herself. All the houses on Mathilda are roomy; Aunt Mary's kitchen is one of the nicest-sized I've ever seen. The houses on Mathilda have front yards, too, and everyone competes to see who will have the nicest roses. They plant petunias and geraniums in boxes and set them on the ledges of their front porches. I always see at least one Italian woman sweeping her sidewalk when I walk down Mathilda. Way down the end Mathilda runs into Penn Avenue. Penn runs past the Allegheny Cemetery. A big old tower made of dirty stone is by the iron gates of the cemetery's entrance. Penn gets into Garfield if you go right; I turn left and walk up a little to Pearl Street and turn down there.

The houses on Pearl Street are row houses; every one seems to be painted red and green. They don't have any front yard of course but they make up for it by having gardens in the back. And they grow all those different kinds of lettuce—even the one with the curly edges that tastes like orange rinds. Sam's mum puts it in salad with wine vinegar and it makes me sick. They grow a lot of tomatoes, too. But not much cabbage. One place has a beautiful garden of gladiolas; they're all pink, yellow, and red. The sidewalks on Pearl are even closer than the ones on Mathilda. In the evening the people come out and sit on the steps of their little concrete porches and talk.

There are a lot of streets like Pearl, with the row houses and the gardens in back. Taylor runs next to Pearl, and LaScelta next to Taylor. Narrow alleyways cut through all three streets; they're only about one and a half cars wide, made of Belgian block. Back in the alleyways the oldest Italians live. Some still don't speak English too well; of course Sam's mother doesn't either. The old widows wear nothing but black, and they wear black babushkas that cover most of their heads. Sometimes a few gray hairs stick out at the sides. They don't have many teeth left. One woman—I can never say her name right, Enriketa or something—is always pulling weeds around her roses and lettuce. I've been passing her almost every day now for two weeks and she always stops to talk with me. I've decided she's in her nineties at least. Of course I don't understand a word she says but she knows Sam's mother. She'll throw her hands around my face and call me *cara* and run in to get me a glass of water or have me sit down on her porch. She has a hideous-looking black cat so I don't stay long. Sam tells me Enriketa came over with his mother from Abruzzi. Says she's a *pie-sian*. But I thought they were all *pie-sians*.

Down at the intersection of Enriketa's alleyway and LaScelta is a beautiful grotto of the Blessed Mother. Ivy and blue morning glories grow all the way up its sides. There are geraniums and white roses at the base. Everyone has those blue and white statues of the Blessed Mother in their gardens but this one is three times as big as any other, and made of marble. The statue is about five feet high; I think they brought it from Italy. I forget the name of the family who owns the grotto but everyone puts cut flowers around the Virgin's feet. Once some one scribbled graffiti around the statue; all the widows were out that day in a rage, scrubbing with nine buckets and brushes.

Down LaScelta a half block is Gebek's, the only place I can find fresh *kiełbasa*. They get it from Polish Hill, about a mile away. Mum says it's okay; I like it. They have fresh ducks and some days even keep the blood so you can make *czarnina*. I'll have to get the recipe from my mum, but I don't think Sam likes it.

LaScelta crosses Friendship Avenue, the street that continues up and circles the square. Sam's Uncle Alfred lives with Aunt Emily on Friendship at the corner. Alfred and Emily are first cousins. Emily's first child died; her second is slow. Sam's family doesn't seem to talk about it much; my family does. Friendship's old; the sidewalks are all broken up and weeds grow between the cracks. There's a pile of rubble where they tore down Sam's old church.

I walk up Friendship to the square again and cross over to South Pacific. The same old trees they cut down on Liberty they left standing on South Pacific. They're sycamores, the kind whose bark is always peeling and leaving yellow marks underneath. At the beginning of the century this end of Pacific was a pretty ritzy place; you can tell because the houses are so big. I counted sixteen windows on the side of the corner house. A Protestant woman named Missus Hegley lives there with four cats. I can smell them when I pass by. She rents out the upper floors to two other ladies. The houses on the left of Pacific are up a little higher than the ones on the right. Pacific is pretty wide and a lot of people have cars. Our pink and white Chevy sits in front of our place—half a black from the corner. The tree by our apartment is dying; it has some kind of disease and they're coming next week to take it down. Our apartment is the third floor of a yellow brick house. Missus Mascili's our landlady, a friend of Sam's mother. The first week we were there Missus Mascili made us dinner almost every day, unless of course Sam's mother did. Missus Mascili still gives me vegetables from her garden: tomatoes, peppers, lettuce, broccoli, and basil. I don't know what to do with the basil; I think they use it in sauce.

The three flights just about kill me after a long walk. I get to the top and sit by the window for a while before starting dinner. Sam comes home late after school and work, about eight o'clock.

Tony

When I fell into bed that night after a muggy day—the kind when paint sticks to you like a magnet and you can't wipe it off—I kept seeing that scribble in my head. It was in the hallway, on my right as I was pulling up the drop cloth, just beside the steps. I was in a hurry to have a beer, so I only saw it from the corner of my eye. Trouble is, I don't really remember what it said. The letters were only half there, like a wartime code. Damn, I thought, I had already given it the final coat. How could I have missed dabbing over a bit of graffiti when I'd primed it?

The hallway was pink now. That's what she wanted. But I'm sure she didn't want some kid's prank showing through those cleaned up walls. So I thought I'd touch it up the next day before I started on the other rooms.

There were a couple other spots I'd missed—must've been tired, or in a hurry because of the heat. So I opened the can of pink and brushed them over, including the graffiti. I didn't bother to find out what it said. Pen ink can be a hard thing to cover up. I wonder how it was that she didn't see it all those years. Maybe because it was behind the table lamp.

Those rooms I painted belonged to my sister. She is my oldest sister, a widow now with grandchildren. She's always treated me swell, even though she got married and moved out of our house when I was just seven. I remember her coming over then, before she started having her own kids, to help my mother. If our father had whipped my bottom she would take me away for ice cream. That ice cream tasted real good.

It's funny about colors. They can follow you anywhere, even to bed at night when you start seeing them over and over. Some people pick real doozies. I didn't say anything about that pink because I didn't want to upset Gen. It didn't turn out so bad anyway. Last summer an Italian family had me paint their windows and awnings red and green. Just like their goddam flag I guess.

After work I go home and wash up, then I go to the bar downstairs and have a beer or two. I like the way the beer looks in the glass before I drink it, with the light shining through it.

I just like to look at things. I don't need to talk much. And I was never very good at schoolwork. How do people pay attention to all those pages in books when there is so much to look at elsewhere? I wish sometimes I could write my own book—a different kind of book—about all the colors I see. No one else seems to notice them. Why is that?

The day after I painted out the graffiti in Gen's pink hallway it came back. Boy was I mad. I took a brush and loaded it up with primer and hit it again and again, until there was no trace of it left. Then, after it dried, I topcoated it with pink for one last time.

Gen loved the color. I got used to it, sort of matched the red rug. The upstairs rooms I painted light green for her. She was getting ready to move in our nephew and his new wife.

I used to live in the attic of that house. Margaret Street was a little quieter than where I live now, but it wasn't right for me to stay there with Gen's family. I felt like a mouse hiding up there. So one day I told Gen that I'd found a place in South Side, where most of my work is anyway. I don't need much room. I don't bother anyone, and no one bothers me.

People wonder why I'm so quiet. And truth is, I never thought of myself that way. As a child I made as much noise as anyone. I looked up to my brothers, and together we got into our share of trouble. But it seemed that I always got stuck holding the buck. I wasn't as good at running away, or figuring out how my father would react. I would just stand there, looking at things, like the mess we made. So I got whacked on the ears a lot.

I tried helping out at home, maybe cleaning up the kitchen or sweeping the sidewalk, but somehow my mind always got the best of me, and I ended up inspecting the broom, or lining up the dishes in different ways. That's when they started calling me "slow" or "different." I didn't mind, because it *was* slow to look at everything the way I did.

I'm glad those days are over. I like painting houses better than sitting in a schoolroom. I don't mind that I never finished high school. It was an ugly building. Nobody cared to fix it up like I would have.

A few years ago I met a woman named AnnaMay. I met her right downstairs here in the bar. She was just sitting there kind of quiet and having a beer right next to me. Then, all of a sudden, she turned to me, pointed at the TV, and said, "Look at the titties on that one. Like two Hershey's kisses." I don't remember the show, but she was right—the girl had almost nothing, while AnnaMay had jugs the size of melons. She also weighed about three hundred pounds.

AnnaMay didn't often come to the bar. She was celebrating her birthday that day. She had come from work too, as a cook at Saint Joe's hospital. Boy though was she pretty. We met up a few times after that. I took her to dinner at Sarah's Restaurant and we shared an apple cake for dessert.

Now my family didn't believe me when I said I was getting married. "What for?" my brothers said. "Well, for companionship." I answered. "And why shouldn't I?" So I did it, and I was never sorry. AnnaMay moved into my apartment, and we'd sit at the bar downstairs and talk about everything we'd seen that day: the colors of smoke coming out of the mill across the street and the sunsets they made, the layer cakes she'd baked at the hospital, or the different colors of make-up she tried on for me. AnnaMay noticed everything, like I did. I didn't care if she was fat. Whose business was it anyway?

She actually apologized to me for dying. That is, she said if she'd known about the tumor in her gut she wouldn't have married me. Imagine that. I still visit her at the cemetery. She overlooks the city from Eighteenth Street, and I like to watch the stones shine there when the sun's out. My brothers and sisters looked in on me after that, at least for a while. Then they stopped. Except for Gen.

I started drinking more beers at the bar. Afterward I would just go upstairs and crawl into bed, get up the next day for work, then back to the bar, and start all over again the next morning. I lost interest in colors around that time. I just passed things up like everyone else, like I had blinders on. The only color I liked was the golden yellow of a draft.

I had all Gen's rooms done, and they looked fine. By then I had started liking colors again, and it made me feel good that she liked the colors too. She made me sweetbread and we sat and ate it in her kitchen after I had cleaned up. We were quiet at first. Gen never felt like she had to say something when she was with me—not like the rest of our family. But then she looked at me and said, real nice and quiet:

"I ran in to AnnaMay's sister at the A&P. She says hello."

"I haven't seen her since the funeral. She never bothered much with AnnaMay when she was alive, you know. Hardly anyone did."

"Well."

"I'm just sayin'."

"You never know why people act the way they do."

"That's for sure."

"Mother used to say: 'There are two kinds of people in this world: those that are loved and those that don't know it.'"

"Yeah. Mum loved everybody. Even dad."

"She did. You figure out what I owe you, Tony. I'm going to the bank tomorrow."

"You don't owe me nothin'."

"Git—don't make me mad. I'm paying you and that's that."

"Well okay then. Thanks. I'll work it up."

I went home feeling kinda strange that evening, like I was the only one in the world. It was a peaceful feeling though, not bad.

Next day I went to see Gen and give her my bill. I remember what a nice, cool day it was. Fall was coming. I had been working on a three-story house out in Carrick, painting the trim a nice brown.

Gen's door was open, so I walked right in, and before I could say anything I saw her sitting there in her favorite chair, like a statue. She didn't blink, and I knew she was dead. They say she had a stroke. I went over and gave her a kiss on the forehead.

The day after the funeral I went with my brothers and nephews to empty out her house. We carried the furniture and boxes out and loaded them into Stan's truck. It took a few trips but we got everything out of there and brought it to his garage on Jane Street. I went back for one last time to pick up a few odds and ends—things I could use in my apartment, like the lamp and small table in the hallway.

I stopped to look at the empty rooms before I left, the ones I had painted all those colors that Gen liked. The hallway looked pretty pink with nothing in it but that red rug But over on that small part of wall along the steps, where the table and lamp had been, I saw the graffiti again. It had come through one more time, and no one had noticed it. I walked over and looked at it closely. I wondered who had written it, how long ago. Was it one of Gen's kids, or maybe someone who had lived there before she and her family moved in? The words had looked faint before, and I wanted to get rid of them so bad I never noticed what they said. But now they were all clear, as if they had been written yesterday. They said *I love you,* in dark blue ink. And there was nothing I could do. I had to leave it be.

74

II
AWAKENINGS

Colors

A boy of sixteen lives in the South Hills. He lives a life of schoolwork, beer-drinking, and colors. He thinks of the colors he carries in his clothes, the colors of the classrooms where hours go by, the colors of a girlfriend's hair and complexion, of the wood shop in the school basement, of the new leaves growing on the trees through the hollow he crosses on the way to school.

A world of colors can be brightened by spring. It is spring and the colors are growing in the South Hills and North Hills of Pittsburgh, and this is what makes it easier to cross over the absent boundary between them in the spring: the sense of color spilling over and concealing all that separates the South from the North.

In the North you can still fish the river, but in the South there is a reverence for the woods. For Luke there is a reverence not only for the woods but also for his neighborhood, as he notices a dusty brick road, a loose concrete sidewalk, a new car parked by a shiny young maple, or the beehives in the next backyard full of pollen and honey.

This Friday evening he leaves the house at seven, walks around the park for an hour, and finally drops into the woods with a case of beer and five friends, while quietly watching the sun melt into the opposite hillside. A sudden breeze turns cold, but he does not feel the cold. During these days of color there can be no distraction from the warmth of the day, from his gaze beyond the third-floor window of English class, from the shadows of his friends holding their beers in the woods, or from the painting he does during a Saturday-morning art class.

It's funny. When the alarm rings he doesn't feel at all hung-over. The window bears a light tapping: soft hail turning into drizzle. The rest of the house—brothers, mother, step-father, and sister—still sleeps. This morning's windowlight is the color of an old handkerchief; it clears a wide spot on the rug, still but fading as the room grows brighter.

Today he will drive alone. He, just sixteen, will take the family station wagon to art school without the usual car pool of two other students. The weather quiets him; last night's beer is gone and he feels awake, receptive. He will be able to listen to the instructor and direct his hand with a pencil or brush.

His best friend is not there; she hasn't shown up for weeks. He sits alone on the floor and sketches a female model wearing a black leotard. The other students talk in small groups or work quietly apart; the teacher has left the room. Light pours in and onto the top of his pad. Clouds are breaking outside.

The room fills with soft color; he looks up and sees beige running along the wall near the ceiling; he notices small sketches the college students have put on the wall beneath it. He notices the different layers of dust coating the floor under the high tables, the paint chipped off the cabinet, the highlight of Jenny's and Louis's hair, the thin shadows of leaves bouncing on the floor.

The elevator has a commode in it this week; it's too bad she isn't there to laugh with him about it. There is a pole stuck into it with a foil halo around its top. The walls are dull red and gray. Several students have written life histories on the ceiling. In one corner sits a plastic fish with a bottle in its mouth. The décor of the elevator changes weekly.

Coming out of the building and down the stone steps he feels the warmth of change hitting his face and hands. The breeze turns leaves and then stops, allowing sun to gather on grass and concrete. It is a day for something different; it has been that way since the hail and solitary drive that morning.

He is alone with the car, with newness all around him, with sun on his back and a small concentrated feeling inside, a feeling that he has used up all of his mind that morning but not his heart.

He will drive to her house; he has only been there once, one evening. Now he will see it in daylight, and he will meet everyone she speaks of.

With the window down he drives and wonders if she will be surprised, if she will share the excitement and know why. He feels his face flush: why is he doing this? What will he say later in answer to his parents' questions about where he went? But this only makes him more intent on arriving there; every minute in the car adds to uncertainty.

He comes from the South; she lives in the North.

He is not too familiar with the road but thinks he remembers the way. He is not familiar with the way the long avenues broaden downhill, or with the bridges that cross the Allegheny River. He is only familiar with the car, and must read signs.

He must ask himself why he feels calm inside, why the colors in the North are higher, broader, than those in the South. And what is it that makes it seem so far away—merely crossing a bridge, a short distance from the art school, which is already practically in the North? Is the distance something to see or feel; is it within him or outside him? Does she know the distance, the part that is inside and the part that is outside?

He arrives. She lives across the street from a convent faced with rich trees, trees of the North which seem to him more independent of one another, each growing as if there were no others. She is not there but her mother remembers him and invites him in. Where is she? Play practice.

Would he like to wait.

Well—

The door opens and she is there. He feels that she knows the excitement, that she is glad he came. She walks over to him and has a lot to say; she always has so much to say. She tells him about the practice, and about her plans for the rest of the day. And she is surprised to see him; she prepares lunch for the two of them as her mother drinks coffee and the younger children come and go. Ten live in that house.

He stays for most of the afternoon, helping her carry boxes out to the porch for dress rehearsal, helping her look for things in the attic, even sitting and talking with her for a while on the front steps.

Then she must get ready to leave. The excitement of the day has almost left him, but the day is still sunny and it occurs to him that he still does not know why it was so unusual for him to come here. And must he go straight home?

No.

You know, he says to her, I have a grandmother who lives over there across the river. I only see her once or twice a year. Maybe I'll drop in on her—can I use the phone?

Of course.

He looks up the number in the phonebook, and asks the mother to keep her children quiet because his grandmother doesn't speak English very well.

She watches him speak lowly and clearly into the receiver.

"What? Now?" His grandmother says. "You coming now?"

"Yes. I have the car. I can drive now."

He can tell his grandmother is excited that day too. He hangs up and looks back to the girl, feeling the mystery of the day and knowing she feels it too, though not as much as he does.

They say goodbye and she touches his arm the way she sometimes does, and says thank you with her eyes.

The trees and long roads of the North gleam around him as he reflects on the morning and afternoon. Now the afternoon is late and he still doesn't know why but he feels a little lost, as if the distance inside him were great, and he doesn't know what he is distant from. Or as if there has always been something missing inside him, a place to be filled by whom, by what, or what place? The morning drive, alone in the light drizzle, had made him aware of this. Maybe that was the reason he went to see her, went all the way into the North, beyond the river, to be with a friend who tied him to something different, something that might fill the gap.

He has two brothers and one sister, and he has been close to each of them at different times growing up, but he has noticed that they have their counterparts in the family; each has someone in the family with a like personality, with some interests to share, things to laugh about. And he has laughed often and enough for his family to hear him, but not enough to clear all the laughter out of him.

He crosses the bridge again; this time the sun is almost facing him, lighting up the close rooftops of the hillside neighborhood where his grandmother lives, very close to the art school, though he had never realized it before.

She is there looking out of her third-floor window as he pulls into her narrow street. He doesn't wave; he must think about where to park. He finds a spot five row houses away from hers. After closing the car door he looks up and sees her waiving. He looks down for a moment and thinks: what will they talk about?

"Wait. I throw away the key."

He looks up again and sees one arm waiving; a wrapped handkerchief falls from her hand. Inside it is the key.

He unlocks the door. Her landlady sits down the end of a long dark hall. She waves and her voice is clear: "Your grandma, she wait for you." He is surprised that she knows who he is. Then his grandmother's voice booms down from above:

"Luca."

"Yeah. Here I come"

He takes the two flights two steps at a time; she begins before he reaches the top: "Luca, how you doing? I'm so glad you come-a see me before I die."

He stops on the landing and stoops to kiss her.

"Thanks God my grandson come-a see me today!"

She limps slightly and is not much over four feet tall. He smells chicken and garlic frying and peeks around to see the yellowed kitchen he barely remembers having seen as a child, before his father died.

She is busy, looking through jars of preserved peppers, washing endive, and saying how surprised she was to know he was coming. "You drive now? Yeah?"

He nods and smiles, and sometimes says, "What?" And she replies: "I know. I'ma Chinese." And they laugh. She is from central Italy.

He walks softly to the other room, the bedroom, to study old photographs and an antique clock that sits on a chest. Behind it is a mirror, and though he doesn't touch it he knows it is warm. A short breeze pushes out brittle lace curtains; a mourning dove sits outside on the telephone wire.

"Luca!"

He quickly turns and re-enters her wide kitchen. He has forgotten the day and the reason he came. The meal is yellow, red, and green, and it smells wonderful. He bites into the endive and vinegar burns his mouth. The chicken is half garlic, the red peppers soft and oily. He has never had food like this.

"Where is the bread?" he asks. She pushes herself away from the table and hobbles over to a tin cabinet. The bread is wrapped twice in plastic bags. She carries the cut loaf back to the table, and watches him eat.

"I no know if you like."

"It's good," he says.

She smiles, nods, and says: "Eh." Then, "Your mother, she know you're here?"

"Yes. I called her."

His lips are red from the peppers and vinegar. He rinses his mouth with ginger ale, but the mark doesn't leave. He will carry it with him until the end of the day.

"I'll do the dishes," he says after they have finished.

"What," she says. "I no do." She waves to the window. "Throw away!"

He laughs again. Her face turns red again too from laughing, then settles back into its seriousness. There is nothing to talk about, but it doesn't seem to bother them. He carefully studies the room while she is left to think.

She thinks she sees him there, her son, and wants to tell him not to be home too late, not to play boxing, not to run around on the roof. Though her grandson's eyes are not the same color as his, their hands and shoulders are the same.

"You know what I'ma think about now?" she says. "Your father."

He blushes; he hadn't really thought about his father that day.

"Maybe it's a time to go, eh?" she adds.

He leaves her calling after him at the top of the stairs, repeating the Italian phrase she has taught him. He must repeat it to the landlady. *Ho mangiato bene sopra alla casa di nonna mia.* I had a good meal at my grandmother's. He says it over to himself all the way down the long stairs. *Ho mangiato bene sopra alla casa di nonna mia. Ho mangiato bene sopra...* The landlady is standing near the bottom of the stairs: a stout woman with a pallid face who speaks even less English than his grandmother. He repeats the phrase perfectly for her and she bows, the way all the old people bow who know his grandmother.

He closes the screen door gently; the landlady pushes the other door slowly and he hears it click as he steps down to the walk, to an unfamiliar place in the North, to a place he had once seen as a small child but could not really remember. It has been a day of places in the North, and now he is on his way back to the South, back to the direction of the setting spring sun, to the place he will always remember best, though he will be back to visit the places he's seen today. Many times he will be back to gather in the places of the North, the way his grandmother gathers in the future and past.

Tracings

Sean

I have been watching that family, their comings and goings, the dark soup they eat, the polite way they scold one another, how intent they are on being different from one another. The girls are pretty and the lads are sturdy. Their father likes a nip of the liquor, it's true, but I cannot say he neglects them. And all are under the watchful, worried eye of the prayerful mother. 'Tis a pity they're not Irish!

Theirs is the house I first slept in after I maintained a good wage in this city. Though I did little more than sleeping there, it was also the background of my dreams, which filled the air daily, and helped me last as long as I did. Everything I saw in those days, from the cobblestones I lifted and set to the thicket of green swooping down the hillsides in August, played over and over in my head until I had no recourse but to sketch them. So my visions mounted, becoming so severely crowded that I couldn't bear any more.

The work I did with my hands became second nature to me, an escape from my prison of images. Often I worked longer and harder than the others, and they would scorn me for it. Was it that I wanted to ground myself in the material world, where there was order?

That was nearly a hundred years ago, though well I remember it, for all the images I tried to fight off when I was alive are now with me forever.

So it is that I am most fond of the young man in that house who likes to draw, for I see in him a reflection of me, and I want him to realize much sooner than I that his gift is to be cherished.

Adam

At around 3:15 this morning the coal burned down and my dad woke Carl and me to go down to shovel it. But Carl just turned over and said, "Your turn." So I did it alone. Some days I don't mind, even if it's a school night. The worst part is when you hit the cold cellar floor, but then you warm up from the shoveling. Some days I hear my mother getting up to use the toilet. But this morning she did not get up. I was the only one alive, it seemed. I sat down on the stool and watched the coals glow. Every now and then blue flames would rise, then disappear. I wished I had my drawing pad. But how could I draw this? It was not just a pile of burning coals; it was the dead of night, the ghostly cellar, and me being a part of it. I would see it all during the next day, interrupting my concentration at school.

Sean

A Monday morning, and I wonder if I am still drunk. My head hurts only a little, but my feet are unsteady. The walk down to the riverside does me good. It's a foggy morning, and mist rises over all the river, from our shore to the steep cliffs on the other side. Will and Padraig meet me in line, and together we board the steamboat.

I stand at the rail and let the mists brush my face, trusting the captain knows the way through this gray cloud. I feel I am sailing through heaven, and waking that day for a second time.

But then we reach the distant dock, where huge piles of railroad ties await us, freshly cut and full of splinters. The sun is already burning through, hanging red in the hazy sky. The drink has made my limbs a bit numb, but my mind has been cleared. I would rather be here, out in the elements, than anywhere else.

Will is full of stories and wants to talk, but I just want to do my work: setting the ties and leveling them where the new tracks will run.

We're working along the river, and as I go I catch its glassy surface, where the fog has lifted but refuses to go away. For some reason the smell of tar does not bother me, nor my blackened hands, nor the sweat on my back. I am thinking that beer does one good.

After lunch most of us slow down a bit. The sun is hot now, reflecting off every leaf of the hillside trees, giving them a silvery glow. I look at the perfect line of black ties we've laid, as if we've cut a hole right through time. For a minute I lose myself, staring at the ties, the silvery trees, and the mirrored river. Then I hear a man's voice—loud—a cry like no other I've ever heard.

At first this sound shattered the picture I saw before me, then it became a part of it. Next I saw men running toward the stockpile—the ties had cascaded. I saw them fallen and strewn about, though I hadn't heard it happen. All I heard was the man's voice.

And then—how?—I knew that voice belonged to Will. I moved in the direction of the commotion, though I could hear nothing but the echo of his voice, which had since ceased. They uncovered him and I saw his face, which was not terrified, but empty and still. I backed away, stunned as I was, and the others let me go, knowing the two of us had been friends.

At the end of the day I lay in my bed, and nothing could replace what I saw in my head: the silvery trees and hazy sunlight casting their light on him, who had died so beautifully young, like many others of my race. It was a strange feeling I had then, that I felt more alive than I had that morning when I boarded the steamboat with my unsteady legs and cloudy head. For it was Will, loud Will, that I wished I could draw with my charcoal, though it would take me a lifetime of remembering to get the features right, and the spark behind his eyes.

Adam

Carl is the better athlete, though it's not for my lack of trying. There were times when I hated him for it, but I could never say anything about it, because I've overheard him bragging about me to his friends—about how well I can draw. It's really my dad who might be disappointed in me; I can feel it. He likes that I do well in school, I think. But he never says so. My mother's the one who sometimes asks to see my work, but she wasn't happy to find out that the nude model we've been drawing for the last couple of months lives up the street.

My sisters aren't artistic either, especially Laurie, who would rather play basketball. What if she had a kid some day who was more like me?

Carl lets me tag along with his buddies, and tries to make me fit in with them. Mostly I'm quiet; I'm thinking about lines, the lines of their faces against the sky, or the lines of the houses that stagger down the hillside where we walk, the patterns the bricks and cobblestones make, the continuous lines of the broken horizon over the city. It's lines that interest me. In bed at night I let my finger remember them and trace them in the air. I've drawn whole worlds in the air above my bed as Carl slept.

Sean

I see life differently now, now that I am only here to observe it. In every house I enter, I see not just a moment in time, the way the living see, but all times at once. Rooms connect sorrow and mirth, the years of upbringing as well as the years of departure. I see the quiet of Sunday morning and the bustle of Christmas Eve; the stillness after an argument, and the bedtime embrace. I see that it is all, in some way, good, though the living (as I once did) refuse to acknowledge it. I am sure it has something to do with seeing, studying everything around you always, in great detail. For in the world you see there are hints of the world just underneath, the one you don't see but may come to know just as well.

It's my world I'd like to share with them, if they'll let me back in to theirs for a wee bit of time. It's the seers, the artists, who will most likely be agreeable to that. This Adam, of the Polish family now living in my former home, is one of them.

Adam

Carl told me about his plan last night. He said he can't wait another year, that he'll sign up and lie about his age so he can get his share of "Krauts and Japs." What could I say? He's done some pretty stupid things before but this time I felt a little proud of him, and wished I could do the same. But they'd never believe me; I'm only fifteen. Who knows though, if the war drags on, I might be joining him.

My dad pretended to discourage him from going through with it, even though he was already signed up. My mom went to church to light a candle. And within a week he was gone. His bed remained unmade next to mine, and several nights I fell asleep staring at it, feeling unprotected.

I board the street car at 7:10 every Saturday morning, holding my bag of pencils, erasers, and charcoal by the tips of my fingers, using the same hand that steadies the tablet under my arm. Today it is cold, cold even for March. Carl has been away for two months.

The streetcar is warmer, barely, and not very full. I can lay the tablet and sack down next to me and fold my arms. I love these Saturday morning rides, the only time I get to see the streets opened up, free of people and too many cars. I watch the glint of cobblestones, and when they're wet, their reflections of the sparks flying off the wires. As long as I'm on the streetcar I have nothing to do, and that suits me fine.

As we approach the museum a cold wind rocks the car. I almost don't want to get out, but class starts in ten minutes. I step back into the cold, though the sun is breaking through the winter haze. I take my time climbing the blackened steps of the museum. Once inside, the dim entryway gives way to dinosaur bones and then stuffed birds.

Mr. Fitzpatrick begins the lesson, lecturing on the Flemish school, and afterwards we follow him to the gallery, where we sit on the floor with our pads, copying the masters. Inside the museum, the weather is always the same. The smells of my carbon and gum eraser are always the same, the smell of my manila tablet and the smell of everything ancient: the bones, the marble columns, the sculpted ceiling. Was there ever a present here, ever a time that was not frozen and lifeless, a pause from everything that fell into my mind at school, church, and home?

As I draw, I lose myself and become part of the pause. It's something I can't share with my family, something that is only mine. My tablet is a trove of gifts. I study it when I am home, alone, wondering if it is possible to live that way—outside of time, always, as a creator.

Mr. Fitzpatrick comes by to critique my drawing. Everything he says is indestructible, like the Bible. When he speaks everyone else in the room disappears. Our conversations our like that, week after week.

After the two hours are over I realize I am hungry, but I must ride the streetcar back home to have lunch. I protect my tablet under my arm, taking care that the pages are secure. I am holding the masters, each frozen in his own time, under my arm as I wait in the cold March wind for my streetcar.

Sean

Sometimes I know the future—not everything all at once, but certain events that relate to my station here. I didn't ask for it; it just happens. I've seen them going off to war for two generations now. I've watched them walk out of their homes, tall young men with straight backs and empty faces, more like spirits than the living. I can see which of them is marked, who will never come home. Then I see their empty rooms in their houses, their beds made perfectly by vigilant mothers or wives, objects set gracefully about, never to be touched again. I am mysteriously tied to the events of this town, and to those who have lived here, especially those who have laid footsteps over mine.

The souls of the Polish boy and mine meet when he steps outside of mortal time, when he is free of conscience and obligations, as when late at night he opens his drawing tablet, and we study his sketches together. I am there too when he sketches in the air, as he falls asleep, and the things of his world become equalized, none good or bad, kept or rejected. I am there to strengthen him, I know, so that he may bear the news of his brother's death in that other world he reads and hears about, the one where people choose sides and pay with their lives.

Adam

Carl has been gone a year now, and dad says the war is going to end soon. We've gotten a few letters from him. They were censored, but still we could see that he was able to think straight, and that he hadn't lost the will to go on. I think he may be a hero someday. I'm sure of it. We don't know exactly where he is, somewhere in the Pacific.

In school many of us have brothers in the war. Their names are on the corkboard, and if one falls the teacher puts a gold star by his name. That's what the government does too: they give the family a gold star to put in the window.

School is mostly the same during a war, but it is also not. We seem to be more serious. Even the troublemakers end up apologizing more often than not, and trying hard not to be so different. I see quiet drama everywhere, as if life has been muffled, and we must rely more on our eyes to sense it. I want more than anything to be able to draw it, to put down on paper all the things I see in people's faces, because I know this time won't last forever, and then I'll no longer find it. In a way, even though it is horrible, our time makes us see more. I think it makes an artist of everyone, and every place where people meet becomes a canvas. I imagine the war itself is also a canvas, a stage of human frailty and tragedy unlike any you could find in peacetime. I wonder if I could ever paint that.

Sean

It was Will's death that changed me. It changed me from being someone who wanted to match everything I saw in this world to something I had already pictured in my head to someone who let himself discover things as they truly are, and only as I presently saw them. That was a great burden to let go. It made me realize that it didn't matter where I lived—in America or in Ireland—because the world was always the same. In it were rivers flowing early morning like moving mirrors, men fitting wood and stone together to fashion places that allowed them a place to sleep, women so beautiful they could steal your breath, and coffins borne on the shoulders of the sturdy living as they walked together in mystery. Lucky for me I died in freedom, unchained to judgments of what is good or bad in what I saw of life.

Now I see even more clearly, more openly, what earth has in store. She moves along as helplessly as her children, though she is blind. Only we are gifted to see.

Adam

A warm day, the end of February. I want to walk home slowly, to catch the scent of spring trying to escape the hold of winter. Already I feel the sun on my shoulders, pressing through my coat, before a cloud pushes it back. I think about other springs, about where the blooming trees are. Mr. Sobieski's yard? Does he have the big cherry tree? Or is it Miss McDonough? I play a game; I try to think in Latin, though I've only studied it for one year. I think I can at least name things. *Nimbus,* cloud. *Arbor,* tree. *Oculos,* eye. I wonder if the world looks different in Latin. It does! Everything is new and fresh, waiting to come out of hiding. *Ver,* spring.

I turn the corner to walk down our street. The sun keeps coming and going, somehow making all the wooden row homes look like one long home, where everybody lives: the Cichowskis and Wawrzeniaks and Komlenics, as well as the others we never got to know very well. The outline of the houses is continuous; it meets the outlines of the bricks in the road, now darkened by a cloud, and then continues to the other side of the street, running along those houses too, before connecting with the elegant bare trees leading up the hillside.

The light is growing dim. The whole world before me is a sketch, its colors muted. Along our narrow street all the windows are closed. It is still winter. Curtains are drawn to keep the heat in. All the windows are rectangular, growing dark before people turn on their lamps. They are dark, dark. Except ours. Our window has something different in it, out of place, unique on our street. I see it now; I'm getting closer, but I stop. I see it now. It doesn't dim with the afternoon. It doesn't go away. It belongs to another world, that one we've been hearing about but never see. It is a bright, golden star freshly set against the pane. It makes my heart stop, my breath burn. My feet turn to stone.

Now I see people entering our house, spying me standing mute on the sidewalk three doors away.

Adam! Adam!

I hear the cry. But I will not move. I want to go back to that other world, mine, the one that painted a continuous picture for me.

Out of nowhere, a hand touches my shoulder. I spin around; no one is there. I feel the hand; it sends a pulse through me that makes my feet move. They move so quickly I arrive at our doorway before I can blink. My mother throws her arms around me, and though I am bleary-eyed I begin to see again: the room full of people, people who are bringing a painting to life.

I collapse into a chair and begin to sob. I am now in the painting, something I can see even though my eyes are covered by both hands.

That night my fingers do not trace the air. I let the quiet night trace me; the winter and the spring, the stars and the clouds, my brother and his hushed voice, tracing me in silence.

A Chill in the Hollow

That was the winter I never needed a winter coat. I had a fall jacket, burgundy, which I wore all the way into March. I'm not sure if it was the weather, or the color my jacket, or the things I kept in my head that winter that kept me warm.

I say the things in my head, yet they would not have been there if I hadn't first heard them. The world is a cauldron of music, and its notes drive into my memory, whether I acknowledge them or not.

Some notes play melodies, others bass lines. And then there is percussion, my hands and feet tapping uncontrollably in calculus class. That year it was Gershwin and Satchmo. Everything I saw that winter, I saw through their eyes.

The rest of my family is not musical. My mother can't sing. My father stares at hymnals in church. My younger brother's taste runs from clangy electric guitar to pep chants at basketball games. And my sister—well—she's the first to pull out Andy Williams at Christmastime. It's not that I fault any of them; they hear their own music. But I often wonder if it infuses everything they do. Do they remember days according to what music was running through their veins? Does a particular song unify the details of another chaotic day, and turn it into a calm landscape? I wish I knew.

It's impossible not to hear what's going on in every corner of our house. My sister will turn the radio or T.V. on in every room she finds herself in, then exit. My mother will spontaneously shout a command and expect you to hear it, wherever you are. My father is more of a grunter, but once he has taken over a room with a project, can't go in there. And where is the stereo? Right smack in the epicenter of our first floor, against a wall in the well-traveled dining room, beside the steps. It's a Zenith console job, and sounds decent, but you can't take it with you, like a transistor radio.

But why would I want to listen to *Porgy and Bess* on a transistor?

I've kissed girls. For a while I would have kissed every one of them if I could: cornering them at parties after we'd drunk beer, safely tucked away in the back of the school band's bus, in a quiet stairwell after the bell has rung. They come in so many interesting looks, so many lovely smiles and turns of the head. What's a 15-year-old to do? I was flooded by them—everywhere I looked, everything I thought, every night I dreamed. Then I fell in love.

She was in my biology class, with dark hair and eyes, a forehead that showed what she was thinking, cherry-tasting lips. Her voice was what slayed me though, softly determined, like a whisper through fog. It lasted about a year. We kissed until our lips were raw. I buried my nose in her hair, held her warm hand, held her as close as I could. Then she slipped away.

I think if it hadn't been for Regina I wouldn't have been drawn to *Porgy and Bess.* I wanted the ache that I found in their voices. I wanted it to drive down into the depths of me, because that's where Regina was.

I had sung many a sappy love song to myself; some of them I actually liked. But I had never heard anything so beautiful as Porgy and Bess singing "Bess You Is My Woman Now" on that LP. It was so much better than the slight version that was buried in our concert band medley, where I'd first heard it. Was my love for Regina even a tenth as beautiful and poetic? I thought every cell in my body went limp as I listened to that song. I finally realized why we were alive.

Walking to school early mornings that winter, with my burgundy jacket and the wind blowing through it, I had nothing on my mind but melodies. The clouds were a melody; the wide steps leading up the hillside were a melody. The trim colors of the brick homes I passed were melodies, as were the footsteps of the other kids I passed on the way. The last flight of long steps leading up to the baseball fields and tennis courts sent crescendos through me: trays of sunlight crashed there, and I could feel the timpani as I walked through.

Sometimes I imagined my clarinet part in my head. My part was almost always a flurry of notes in the background, but I liked that. They might sound complicated, but to me they were like walking. Most of the time I would go on hearing melodies throughout the day, at least until the fifth or sixth period, when I would start nodding off in class.

It never occurred to me that everyone else wasn't hearing music too. How could they miss it? Or maybe it was that they had never studied music, or never heard *good* music, so they were doomed to go about deaf to the world's notes. That was disturbing.

Even more disturbing was watching people fall prey to anger and bitterness, or even loneliness and boredom, without knowing that all they had to do was find some music to lift them out of it.

That summer I spent a lot of time in my room, reading and painting pictures. I also went out with my friends, hung around at the park, and worked at the corner store as a stock boy. I would see Regina from time to time, noticing that she had grown more womanly and even more beautiful in the space of a few months. She didn't seem to want to speak to me though; her face had become a little stern and withdrawn. By autumn I found out that her brother had died that past June—a drug overdose of some kind, one of those things people don't talk about.

I tried to forget it. I tried to forget her face. But I couldn't help remembering the old one, the one she had worn before tragedy, the one that smiled on cool nights and looked at me sideways in biology class. So I walked home from the park at the end of a cool autumn day and found the creek's water trickling through the hollow, and a slight wind rustling the tree-of-heaven trees. It seemed a longer walk than usual. The hill leading up to the alley behind our house seemed steeper, unfamiliar. I passed the set of bee hives our neighbor kept, and saw the darkening sunlight pass through clouds of honey bees settling in for the night. The grass at my feet smelled of snakes and grasshoppers and bitter weeds. There was only one light on in the house; it shone through the small kitchen window.

Inside I could find no one but my sister, and unusually, the house was quiet. My brother was staying at a friend's.

"Where's mom and dad?" I asked.

Her eyes became red in an instant, but she held back any tears. She was like that.

"Mom isn't sleeping here tonight.

"Why?"

"I don't know. Dad just said she wasn't sleeping here, then he left too."

"But why?" I repeated. I could already feel my heart rising to my throat. Katie looked away. For the first time I could remember, my confidant, ego-driven sister looked lost.

"They had a fight," she said. Then: "Luke, did you ever notice dad..."

"What?"

"Looking at you funny. Or hiding—"

"Where?"

"Oh, never mind."

Then she too left, on her way to spend the evening with her girlfriends, and probably talk it over with them.

My stepfather came home late; I was in bed, though I hadn't been sleeping. Was it after midnight? I had been lying there listening to the quiet, that almost inaudible buzz that comes from darkness. The shadowy objects in my room—the dresser, book shelves, ceiling lights, curtains—seemed to both protect and threaten me. They were immutable and stationary, while I tossed and breathed aloud.

97

My stepfather was a kind but unknowable man, like a bus driver whom you trusted to get you there, though you had no say by what route. My siblings and I barely knew him, but we loved our mother, and so we kept up our part of the bargain. So it was earth-shattering that my mother would not keep hers. I knew she was a woman, one who had suffered misfortune and pain, one who deserved a second chance, with all its bumps and turns. But she was first of all my mother. Her love had always been unconditional, unlike any love my natural father might have given me: he was dead and gone.

Katie didn't come home. She stayed at a friend's house too, as she often did on weekends. I awoke the following day to a quiet house. I thought no one else was home, but when I came down to get breakfast there was my mother making pancakes, and my step-father busily eating them.

"Morning," I said, not looking much at either of them.

They both replied, flatly, as if out of key. My mother announced that she was going shopping. Did I want anything? My step-father quietly sipped his coffee. It was to be a regular Saturday. Within five minutes she was out the door, and he was off on one of his usual quests to fix something.

Katie returned around eleven o'clock. I asked her softly: "What happened last night?" She merely shrugged, twisted up her mouth a bit, and turned on the radio. Soon a couple of her friends arrived at the door, and her world was filled with chatter.

Mine, however, remained tied to the gravelly notes of Louis Armstrong's "A Kiss to Build a Dream On," which I had been hearing since I'd bought the album *Hello Dolly* at the used record store one weak before. I thought about kissing, the deep kisses I'd had with Regina and the little pecks my mother still gave me. There was Nana's kiss, and then there was my Grandpap's kiss, which came with a scratchy beard. I had never thought about Louis Armstrong's kiss, but it was pretty clear from the song that he had kissed someone pretty well.

We had a full rehearsal the next day, after school, as a final preparation for our concert. It was a nice day, and our attention was divided, but Mr. Burton's baton worked us with its usual magic. I added the flourishes of my clarinet's notes feverishly, excited about the harmonies I made, happy that I was helping to reproduce whatever had been in Leonard Bernstein's mind when he had written those pieces from *West Side Story* that we were playing.

I was glued to the edge of my chair, unable to budge, because I was no longer part of the world of chairs and floors and walls and sunshine. I don't know how I would have reacted if someone had spoken to me, because I felt as though I didn't exist either, at least not all of me. It had all gone to my heart: in there was lodged the music, and the parts of myself I knew only from music. It was a state of bliss, and I was not sure it would ever end. But the practice finished and everyone rose to leave, to destroy the bliss. So I left too.

The walk home felt oppressive, as if the declining sun were piercing me, not comforting me. My legs, stomach, arms, and head were hollow; my feet moved like blocks of lead. Chilly air curled around every curve of my body; it searched out every pocket of warmth and overcame it with its wintry intent. Half-way home I sat on the steps that led me down to the hollow. There was no music down there. Even the creek had been silenced by ice. Families along the hilltops were sitting down to eat. Dogs lay curled on their mats. Everything was far off and unknowable. Migrating birds sat still in the baring trees, clinging to vines. My burgundy jacket turned gray, and gave no protection.

With darkness encroaching, I got up to leave. I left my shadow there on the broken concrete landing and headed up the long hill toward home, feeling warmer now with every step, a warmth that must have come from me. There was no melody in my head, and I waited for one to enter it. But none did.

And so, for the first time, I made up my own.

Doodles

I began doodling in high school, and I'm pretty sure it was the result of boredom. My best doodles were done in chemistry class as I listened to our mechanical teacher, Mrs. Hoffmann, drone on and on to impart information without any hint of its connectivity to our lives. Most of the brains in the classroom were elsewhere, and mine was on the page.

I could never stand a pristine piece of paper. It existed only to be defiled by my pen, to give it some kind of life, not only along its pre-printed lines but in the margins as well. Everything I drew there was a download of my mind, the unguided direction it took, the uncontrollable nature of it amidst the controlling nature of the classroom. Doodles were a form of breathing.

After I realized that doodles played an important role in my life, I began to see life as a doodle. I don't think many others saw it that way; they all seemed so content to draw clean boxes along the straight and narrow, often in two dimensions. My road could go from psychedelic to cubist in a heartbeat, then end up a Kandinsky or Chagall.

The thing about doodles is that their randomness creates a kind of order on the page, a multi-layered world of possibility where you can get lost, and find yourself. So I gave up on the phony order of perfect textbooks and note pages. They always made me feel lost.

I'm assuming people take me for someone who has things under control. I have a calm appearance. Is it because I've given in to the chaos, accepted it and tried to use it as a guide, rather than seeing it as an object of endless scorn? There is very little that surprises, startles, or scares me. I think that is why I survived the night I am about to relate to you.

I was working as a waiter that year, reading in the dark while waiting for my first customers in the cocktail lounge. The restaurant, called The Colonial, was deep in the South Hills of Pittsburgh. We served businessmen mainly, and specialized in the grilled steak. But my domain, being young and somewhat new to the game, was limited to the lounge. There I served drinks and appetizers, listened to our slick Italian piano player, and endured the flirtations of every pathetic living thing that came in.

One muggy summer evening some of the busboys (who were closer to me in age than the wait staff) invited me to have a drink with them. I, the bookish college grad, had little in common with them, but that has never mattered much to me. They were friendly and genuine, and we had all had a rough Saturday evening at the restaurant.

So I met them at Steve's apartment after work, and they were happy I had come.

Steve lived with a couple of other guys, one of them also a busboy. The apartment, just off Route 51, a busy four-laner, looked only as comfortable as the people who happened to be in it. And that Saturday evening it held five of us, all relaxing with beer and a communal joint.

At one point Steve, a puppy-faced guy who seemed to be immune to danger, decided we should all go to a bar he liked in Shadyside, a good half-hour drive away. Why shouldn't we?

By the time we reached *The Pitt* we didn't know what day it was. The world had only been dark, a place where strangers bumped into one another in a cloud of fermented hops, with pinball lights providing fireworks in the background and thumping music keeping our hearts in gear.

We all got lost, though I did succeed in spotting Steve from time to time. He seemed to know everyone, and from what I could tell, everyone was eager to see his puppy-dog face.

I had my eyes on an athletic-looking blonde, or almost-blonde. She had dark eyes and very fair skin, and I noticed she was looking my way. A group of guys stood by her, and she appeared to be taunting them. I found a seat at the bar, knowing she would make her way over there for another drink, which she had already done several times.

I grabbed a napkin and the bartender's pen, and started doodling. I could barely make out what I was drawing, but drew just the same. When I had filled the little square napkin I took another, and filled that one too. I felt I was an invincible artist in the midst of charlatans.

While deep in this reverie I detected a change in the air, a subtle perfume that seemed to blow by. I knew it was her. Before I could think her hand passed by my face, holding an empty beer glass, which she placed on the counter.

"That's nice."

"'Scuse me?"

"Your drawing. It's nice."

"Oh, thanks. Here, you can have it."

"Really? Thank you! Are you sure?"

"Yeah. I could make a million of these."

"I'll bet they're not as nice as this one."

"It's just a doodle."

"But I *like* it. I *really like it.*"

"You need another beer?"

"Ah, yeah. I'll have an Iron."

"I think that's all they have here."

I got the bartender's attention and ordered Irons for both of us. I picked up both drafts and handed one to her.

"Cheers."

"Cheers."

I took a long gulp, set my glass on the bar, and the lights went out.

I mean they really went out. No electricity. No music, no lights, no fans overhead. We heard nothing but thunder, then a chorus of "Ahhhh…" when everyone's compromised mental synapses finally fired and figured out what had happened.

Someone opened the door, but the thick vertical strands of rain glowing from car headlights did not look inviting. There was safety in the dark.

I stayed there for a while, inside, holding my glass of beer as others shuffled about me. It was getting pretty warm so I got up and made my way to the door. I wasn't sure how long I'd been sitting there, but I noticed now that most everyone had left.

Outside, where the air was even thicker, I heard loud chatter riding on the misty air. It seemed to come from all directions. So I began walking. Though the street was dark, I caught glimpses of the gleaming asphalt when an occasional car passed by.

I turned down a side street. There seemed to be a party going on there, or several parties all strung into one. Someone called to me from a porch, where a few candles glowed.

Inside, more candles, more bodies, more beer, and, before I could blink, a line of cocaine set before me on a glass coffee table. I passed it up in search of good company. By now I'd reached a state of both exhaustion and hyper-awareness, and I knew, as the joints were passed around, that the next real light I'd see would be daylight. Until then it would be flickering candles and the light of eyes.

Amid the soft murmur of mellow voices in the house I heard another: a loud shout. It came from the walkway in front of the house. I heard it again, then another voice answer it, as if announcing a boxing match. I soon found out, when I exited the darkly-lit house to the sodden front porch, that I was not mistaken. A fight had broken out. Two shadows leapt and swung at each other. One of them belonged to Steve.

"Steve!"

I hopped down the stairs, tripping over the last step and landing right in the middle of the battle. Before I could regain my balance a fist landed on my cheek.

I woke up in a candle-lit bedroom, a room that smelled very nice, though what little I could see of it was swirling uncontrollably.

One thing that wasn't swirling was a girl. She had a cool rag which she pressed to my face. I could only see her shadow, just enough to know that her features were fine and her body firm. She kissed my forehead.

"What about Steve?" I mumbled.

"I don't know about Steve. But you need to...relax. Just... relax..."

I realized the lovely scent of the room was coming from her. I drew her to me. She felt like a silken pillow; her hair tickled my neck. I believe we made love there on a stranger's bed in a darkened house in Shadyside before I passed out again, and awoke without her.

The party was over. Bodies lay everywhere, and I had to step over sleeping masses on my way down the stairs and out the door.

Crickets gave way to birds, for the sky was shedding its shadow in favor of a robin's egg blue. The storm had long abandoned the city, leaving only thin streaks on the horizon. I began walking, trying to remember where I was, where I had been, and what I had to do.

I had to find a way home.

I walked in the direction of Fifth Avenue, hoping to catch an early bus. Did they even run at this hour, on a Sunday? It was odd to see no one about. Not even a paper boy. As I turned the corner onto Fifth I heard a window slam shut—someone had had enough of the newly chilled air.

The avenue, too, was strange without cars moving on it. They were all parked along the curb, the only day of the week it was allowed. I amused myself by finding patterns in the old sidewalk, its random cracks and heaves, along with small angular puddles and drying shadows. For someone who had barely slept, drunk half a dozen beers, smoked pot, and gotten a bruised cheekbone, I felt pretty good, as if I had been drained of all misfortune. And whaddya know, I heard a big old bus gearing up way down the road behind me. I looked up and saw that I had arrived at a bus stop. I dug around for some change in my pocket as the bus approached but never slowed down. Instead the driver gave me the "out of service" wave. I threw up my hands, but off he went into the sunrise.

On his tail, however, came a yellow taxi, which dutifully stopped as the driver nodded: "Need a ride?" I climbed into the back seat.

"Where to?" he said, his eyes centered in the rear view mirror.

"Mount Lebanon. Just off West Liberty. I'll let you know when we get there."

"Sure thing."

I could feel myself dozing off in the stale-smelling car amid the little bumps in the road. The driver spoke, sending a chill through my heart.

"What have you been up to all night?"

"Oh, just a little partying."

"A little? You're just going home now?"

"Yep."

We stopped at a long light at an empty corner, which further increased the silence between us. Then the light turned green.

"Stay at your girlfriend's?"

"Nope."

I expected a reply, but he made none, just drew a deep breath which for some reason made me feel uneasy. I saw the eyes in the mirror again, and they were calculating. The car hummed along down Fifth toward the center of town.

"I was heading for the garage when I picked you up. I wouldn't mind getting some breakfast if you're up for it."

"No thanks."

"Sure?"

"I just want to get home, thanks."

"Whoa. The Liberty Bridge is closed. I'll have to go through South Side. Ever been to that new bar on East Carson?"

"Which one is that? There's only thirty million of them."

"The one up around Eighteenth. It's one of those—you know—depends on what night you go to find what you're looking for."

I began to sweat, and rolled down the window a bit more. We crossed the Birmingham Bridge and I smelled the sulfuric air enter the car.

East Carson was a little more crowded, with some people walking about. Church bells peeled. As we approached the ramp to go up to the tunnels we came to another long light. I dug around in my pockets, pulled out a few bills and handed them to the driver.

"Here you go. Think I'll just get out here."

"What? Here!"

"Yeah. Here you go. Thanks."

I opened the door real fast and got out, slamming it shut behind me. The light turned green and the car behind us started honking, so he pulled reluctantly away, eyeing me again from his mirror.

For the first time in what had seemed an eternal night, I felt alone. A good alone; free of the unpredictable, free of fate, of expectations and human drama. I'd had enough of it, and I was sure I'd find my way home.

But first I wanted to rest, and soak in the beautifully chaotic, man-made and natural environment. I walked under a blackened railroad bridge and smelled the tar and a century of grinding wheels that had rolled above me. I paid homage to the Queen Anne's lace blooming at the bottom of the hillside, its bitter milky smell somehow comforting.

I turned around and saw the aqua-colored onion domes of St. John the Baptist church, its brown brick streaked as if from the charred remains of all the souls that had worshipped there. I walked up the ramp toward the Liberty Tunnels, where I knew the Mt. Lebanon bus would stop. As I ascended the steep, Belgian block road I looked back and saw Pittsburgh rising unevenly across the river, its jumble of eras reduced to an enticing whole, and white and pink doodles streaking the dawn sky above it. It was there I sat on a low concrete wall for an undetermined length of time before the heat returned, and I made my way to the empty bus stop.

National Biscuit Company

My job is taking the little cookies out of their molds and wrapping them up in neat little boxes. At first I was nervous about it. I didn't want to disappoint my father; he took me out of school to work here. I get 25¢ an hour, and I am allowed to pay my streetcar fare and buy lunch once a week for 11¢. The other days I eat an apple or a sandwich from the ham my father brings home under his coat. He says I need it, since I am the oldest and the other nine aren't working yet.

That first day was in November, and it was a cold one. The streetcar was packed, chilly, and filthy. I stood most of the way—a good 45 minutes from South Side to East Liberty. It was also the day I got my period. I prayed to the Blessed Mother that no one would know. When I got home that evening it was dark, and I didn't tell my mother about it.

Greta stands next to me. She was quiet at first. She's small, but I think she's older than me, maybe 17 or 18. I said hello to her and she smiled a little, but looked away. I found out that her English isn't that good. I also found out that she doesn't speak Polish or Lithuanian. Well, she did look up when I tried to say hello in Lithuanian— something my father taught me. That's when I found out she is Latvian, which is almost like Lithuanian, except that Latvians are Lutherans.

Greta and I got into trouble for laughing so much. They said we weren't concentrating on our work. I wanted to speak up and tell them to count all the boxes we'd packed, but I was too afraid. What if they told me to go home? How would my mother manage without my pay?

So I learned to work quietly, letting my mind wander and trying not to think of anything too bad. One thing I could think about was bowling. The tournament was coming up, and last year we had taken second place. Miss Stambroski says we have a strong team this year, and I've been bowling about 180. It's such a thrill to knock down those stubborn old pins. After a good game I feel like I'm getting somewhere, like I've accomplished something. Miss Stambroski is such a nice woman. She doesn't mind if I'm a bit late.

Sometimes they give us animal crackers. The broken up ones. I have a taste for them, but mostly I put them in my pocket and take them home. Besides, I don't like crumbs and want to keep my work bench neat.

I face the windows when I work, and as the light fades I catch my reflection in them. Sometimes I don't believe it's me. My hair looks so dark, like my father's. And I have grown so tall. Just last year I was in eighth grade. Now I am looming over most of the boys my age. It makes me feel awkward.

I want to get to know that girl in the window.

Some days everything gives me a thrill: the streetcar ride through the busy city, the beautiful homes we pass by, the big chestnut tree in the park across the street, the warm light pouring down onto me as I work. Other days I want to cry. And I don't really know why. I can't think of anything in particular that made me sad. Yet I am. I struggle to find words, to say the right thing. On those days I avoid looking at the girl in the glass, because I feel deep down that I have to answer to her. And I can't.

Last night I couldn't get to sleep. I couldn't empty things out of my head, things I had seen that day. It's like I have a moving picture up there that keeps playing over and over. I heard people walking in the street outside our window. I heard my dad come home, stumbling over us to get into my mother's bed, then yanking the curtain across so hard I thought it would come off the rod.

I know what they do in that bed. I say a prayer that he doesn't find me awake. Once I think he thought I was my mother and he tried to kiss me. But I pushed him away and said, "No! Daddy—it's me, Genevieve!" He mumbled something, smelling like beer, and kissed me on the forehead. That's when I started to like being at work more than being at home. It's also when the girl in the window began speaking to me.

She looked at me so matter-of-factly, her finely chiseled face framed by abundant black hair, her blue eyes sparkling in the glass, and I knew what she was saying. I had forgotten the time. When I looked down I was surprised at how many boxes I'd filled. My boss came by, as he sometimes does. He looked at me, then glanced at the window. Did he see her there? Did he recognize us? I felt myself blushing.

For a while I didn't look up. I focused on my work, not on what I was becoming. Some days the future seemed scary. This was one of those days.

I thought instead of Christmas, the little tree we brought into our crowded house, how I would sit up and look at it after the others went to bed, promising my mother I would blow out its candles. I thought of watching my mom make noodles, her face so content as she cut them into little strips. I thought of the pigeons that landed on our windowsills, and the first day in spring that we opened our windows, letting the winter dust fly away. I thought, *is only the past so beautiful? Will I be able to let it go?*

The weather was bad during the streetcar ride home. Rain flew against the windows, and our feet were in small puddles on the floor. I gathered up my skirt to keep it from getting dirty, and buttoned up my sweater. An older boy sat next to me—eighteen or nineteen? I pretended not to see him, but how could I not help noticing his beautiful, dark eyes? The streetcar kept rocking back and forth, and I was sitting on needles, afraid of bumping in to him. Wouldn't you know it then, my stop came before his, and as he pulled his boots back to let me pass one of them caught my skirt and held me in place as I squirmed to pass over him. I felt my face going pink as he said, "Sorry ma'am."

I replied, "It's okay," as I broke loose and ran for the door, never looking back, and sorry I didn't, because I kept looking for his face that evening as I helped my mother in the kitchen. What exactly did his nose look like? His brow, his lips? I had only seen him at a glance.

I dropped the bowl of flour, and my mother just handed me the broom, without saying a word. I know she didn't have time—of course not—how could she, when she had ten mouths to feed? I could not even bring it up; I had to keep it to myself, which was very hard, because there was nowhere I could hide. My sisters knew. Florence said: "What's wrong with Genevieve?" I told her to shut up, which I rarely did, and my mother gave me the cold eye. Still though, she said nothing as she put a cake into the oven. That was our dinner.

I wanted nothing more than to get to work the next day, to smell the warm cookies as soon as I entered the packing room, to see the wall of windows with their warm light pouring in. I set my mind on nothing but packing those neat little boxes. I felt I could do just that forever, that everything would be okay if I kept putting little cookies into little boxes.

Then—about noon—I stopped. My hands froze, and I stared at them for I don't know how long before I heard something—a voice—as if it were under water. *Genevieve. Genevieve.* It was Greta. She touched my shoulders, first one, then both. Her hands felt like nothing to me at first. *Genevieve.*

Yes, Greta.

"Genevieve, it's Mister Heisey. He's coming down the aisle."

I didn't look up, as I usually did when Mr. Heisey passed. I heard him say something to Greta, and she spoke back to him. Then he left.

"Come now, Genevieve. It's time for lunch."

I thought about our lunch conversation on the streetcar ride home. I thought about it because it didn't seem that the words I had spoken were mine. Greta asked me why I had stopped working, and I replied, *Because I don't want to put cookies into boxes anymore.* Why had I said that? What's wrong with putting cookies into boxes, anyway? Greta looked so puzzled, as if I were speaking Chinese. *Your family needs money,* she finally said. I looked at her. I felt I was crying, but no tears came. Then I said, or did I say anything? So many thoughts went through my head. I was a little angry, and sad, but Greta's eyes were so kind I could have spouted off anything and she would have listened.

I wanted to go away, to leave the bakery and my family and the three little rooms we lived in. I wanted to stay on the streetcar to see where it would take me. Was there a world beyond the neighborhoods of Pittsburgh I knew? Was there something my hands could do other than clean and wash clothes and pack cookies? What did people look like in that other world? How would they see me?

My stop had come. I got off and watched the streetcar spark away, up 18th Street toward Mount Oliver, where I had never been. As I approached our home I saw the bushel of laundry my mother had set on the front steps for me to carry in. Where else could she have put it?

The sun was in my eyes as I waited for the 54C the next morning. The air was even clear. A flock of blackbirds flew over, making a lot of noise. And I was back to normal. Along the ride I kept my arms folded. The ghost of me in the window let me know that every hair was in place. I smiled at Mr. Kujawa as he boarded and he nodded back. The ride seemed long, but it came to an abrupt end. I had been daydreaming.

I got off, looking down to mind my dress, hearing the big old car as it jolted away. It was not a long walk to the bakery, and I always liked the chance to exercise my legs after the long ride. I didn't look up until I'd arrived. But what I saw was not familiar. None of my co-workers were in line. And there were so many others there I didn't recognize, though one of them was Mr. Heisey.

"Mr. Heisey! Hello!"

"Good morning, Genevieve."

"What's happening?"

"No work today, Genevieve. And maybe not for a long while. There's been a fire."

Then I smelled the smoke. How could I have missed it? Greta took my arm, out of nowhere. She pulled me over to the edge of the cobblestones, where the park began. I looked at her, but she was not all there: my tears distorted her and everything around me.

"But Mama needs the money," I said. *It's what I have to do. I won't have cookies to bring home now. I'll lose myself! How can I be at home all day...*

Greta put her arms around me and patted my back. I saw figures moving behind her, like painted sticks. But one was not moving. My eyes began to clear and I saw him now, looking at me: the boy I had met on the streetcar. He waited, then smiled.

Secrets

Sometimes I just like to sit. Sometimes I sit even if there is work to do. Usually I'll do that if there is no one else around. It's my own private time, and during that time I go deeper inside myself. Something is calling there. Something wants out.

I didn't think I'd ever have five kids; it just happened. And I like to let things happen. So much is beyond my control. I love each of them, each of their lovely faces and different personalities. If it weren't for them I think I'd be glued to a chair.

When I was growing up sitting was frowned upon. There was always work to do, and anyone who just sat wasn't doing her work. I have two older sisters and two brothers, and most of the work fell to them, so I spent a lot of time in the kitchen with my mother. If my sisters complained that I got to do the easy stuff—measuring out ingredients, slicing bread, or boiling water while they scrubbed floors and beat rugs—my mother stood up for me. *When Violet's older she'll do that too,* she said, though I knew even back then that she didn't mean it.

My mother worked so hard for all of us, but she always made time to sit too. Sometimes she'd sit and say her prayers, and other times, as she got older, she'd sit and crochet. But once or twice—I'm sure of it—I remember seeing her sitting and doing nothing. Just sitting. That was something no one else in the family ever did. Our family was athletic and active: everyone knew we could be counted on to get things done. My brother Carl was captain of the football team. My sister Laurie played basketball. My father was a star gymnast, and my mother quite a bowler. I like to watch sports myself; I was head cheerleader. Those were fun days, so full, no time to sit.

Now the kids are at school, all day. I sent my little one, Amy, off to Kindergarten in September. That's when it hit me. I had too much time to sit. It was the first time in my life I could remember having all that time, all the time in the world. I could set my own schedule, do my chores when I wanted, or not at all. It was an strange feeling, something like freedom, but a little scary too. Things began to snowball in my head, and I couldn't stop them. Old thought and feelings came back to me. I remembered a little drawing I did as a fifth grader. It was a drawing of Saint Catherine. Sister Loretta liked it and hung it on the board. Then an eighth grade boy came by and drew over it with a pen. He made her look cross-eyed. I never felt like drawing after that.

I also remembered a book I had read about Florence Nightingale. I wanted to be like her, to help people that way. But my father said only loose girls became nurses. That was that.

It's not that I am unhappy with where I am. I have a nice little house with an addition we put on with two more bedrooms. My neighbor Christy and I have become good friends. I put up a bird feeder this year. My husband bought me roses for my birthday, and took us all out to dinner.

As my days got longer and seemed to repeat again and again, I felt I needed something to help me turn off my mind. I thought a crossword puzzle might help, but it didn't. I just kept looking up and thinking about anything but the crossword puzzle. So I tried having a glass of wine. At first I could have a glass and keep cleaning or sorting laundry. It seemed to work. So I had another, and kept working. Then I sat down, between loads, just for a few minutes.

Those minutes turned into hours. I could amuse myself by just sitting there, dulled by the wine, listening to the quiet. I heard the house creak, the dog moan, and the birds chasing one another outside.

I never even turned on the TV. If a neighbor came to visit I said I was tired and needed to take a little nap. So my coffee pot didn't get much use.

I went on for months like this, hiding wine bottles in the hamper or behind the flower pots on the back porch. My time, as I used to think of it, was the only time in my life I'd ever felt so free. I didn't have to answer to anyone. No diapers to change, no floors to scrub for my mother, no First Friday masses to attend, no uniforms to wear. It was funny to see how easily my world could fall apart. And there I was, just looking at the pieces, with no reason to pick them up.

I can't complain about my upbringing. If nothing else I can say I always felt loved, and that sense is what keeps me going. I want to be sure my kids can say the same some day. But when I drift off into my time, I feel a tug in the opposite direction, something telling me I can't have my time, not yet. Why is that?

When you are loved you can endure anything, and anything that happens to you falls in the shadow of that love.

Last week Amy found me asleep on the couch. She had woken up with a bellyache, so I let her stay home from school. She had been watching cartoons and playing with her dolls. I had vacuumed and redd up the first floor before lying down, the wine I had drunk making my head spin. I fell asleep thinking of the look I had seen on her face. It was familiar. Where had I seen it before?

Now there she was, looking at me, her little eyebrows wrinkled up and eyes wide—*Get up, mommy!* She kept repeating it, and I heard her, but something kept dragging me down, back into sleep, away from this world. She pulled my arms and touched my face, and those little hands felt like snow. Then I got up. I took her in my arms, and she started to cry.

"What's wrong, honey?"

"I missed you!"

"But I'm here, honey."

"You *weren't* here!"

116

Every year I throw a Christmas party. It's mostly for the family, including many of my aunts and uncles, but a few neighbors also show up. Amy helped me bake cookies this year. She was so attached to me I nearly tripped over her in the kitchen. I watched her intently decorate the cookies with colored icings. She said she wanted to be a baker when she grows up.

I love my Aunt Ethel. I don't think I've ever seen her sad. She wears bright make-up and flowery dresses. As a child I always looked forward to her hugs. She and Uncle Jerry lived way out in the suburbs somewhere, and I remember feeling that my family stretched far beyond my imagination. Now I live in those suburbs, and they come to my house for Christmas instead of my mother's. Aunt Ethel is wearing out, but she still shines. She may be in the early stages of Alzheimer's. It runs in the family.

At some point during the party—I can't say when—Amy hugged me in such a way that I knew something was wrong. She looked at me funny when I gave Aunt Ethel her hug, and then Uncle Jerry. My mother, too, was eyeing us.

I'm sure we all keep secrets. How couldn't we? Our lives are so different. I've always tried to imagine what it would be like to be one of my sisters. And I just can't. Everything I know comes through my eyes. Some things I count as secrets because if I told others about them it would cause hurt. And I see no point in that. But if my secrets are hurting others because they are secrets—that is something else. So right smack in the middle of my Christmas party, the happiest day of my year, when Amy looked up at me and said, "I don't like Uncle Jerry," I felt my breath leaving me; my face went numb. Still, I played along as if I didn't know: "Why not, honey?" And then she started crying.

I took her to another room and held her there. She repeated "I don't like him!" until she fell asleep in my arms. She never saw the tears in my eyes.

I never wanted to share my secrets, but it was shared whether I wanted to or not. I had become a good actress, always smiling and cheerful with Aunt Ethel, giving Uncle Jerry the same hug while never meeting his eyes. I did that for years. *Years.* I tried to teach myself to forget about him, about those days so long ago at my mother's Christmas parties, when he would take me into another room, smelling of beer, and teach me a game I didn't want to play. He did that until I was eleven years old, when I told him *no!* so angrily he stepped back, and never touched me again.

Poor Aunt Ethel, who never had children of her own. How could I ever think of explaining it to her? I think it would have broken her heart. So I let it go. I thought it would go away. But it only settled deeper inside me. And now, with Amy's tears, it came right back to the surface, like an angry bubble about to burst.

I wanted to march out there and slap him so hard he'd fall over. *How dare you!* How *dare* you! But I sat quietly for a few moments to collect myself. I said a prayer. I asked for strength. I would talk first to Father Risco.

"You must find it in your heart to forgive," he said. "Pray for him."

I left the confessional feeling so many things: hollow, a bit angry, scared, sad. I thought if I could have a glass of wine those feelings would go away, and I would not have to question why Uncle Jerry had done that to me, why Amy would have to grow up too fast, why Father Risco's voice had sounded like one from a radio play. I could say an Our Father and a Hail Mary for Uncle Jerry, and not think about who might be saying them for me, or Amy.

But instead I had to drive home. I had to sit at traffic lights and wait for people to cross the street. The drive seemed much longer than usual. It was such a bright, clear day. It didn't seem like January.

As I pulled into my driveway I wondered if I would get out of the car. It seemed such a safe place, my own, not under the influence of anyone but me. Was that a bad thing?

So I sat there. The car was warm inside, and the sunlight fell straight onto my face. I thought, for the first time, sitting there alone in that car, *I don't have to do anything I don't want to do.* No prayers for Uncle Jerry. No protecting Aunt Ethel. No looking the other way when my child is in danger. No more carrying secrets around inside me like lead.

I decided to paint my kitchen, and rearrange my living room furniture. I started the car up and drove to the paint store. It was still early.

By 3:30 the kitchen was painted a bright yellow, covering up the dreary moss green it had been. The new color made my wooden cabinets look richer, and I quickly laid a new coat of wax on the speckled linoleum floor to brighten that up too.

When the kids walked in I put them all to work, helping me heave the couch over to the window from the opposite wall, pushing the arm chairs to a corner where they huddled around my antique round table, and setting the TV at an angle near the bottom of the stairs—a spot I had always felt was under-used. The new arrangement was much homier and welcoming, and the warm kitchen light now had more room to overflow into the living room. My work was done. And I hadn't even had a drop of wine. My heart raced and my head was light. The kids went to their rooms to do their homework. Then I heard Ray's car drive up. I felt my smile widen from ear to ear as he opened the door.

"Honey?"

"I'm here, in the kitchen."

"Hell—oh! What's this? A new paint job? You didn't tell me—"

"I know. It's a surprise. Do you like it?"

"I do. You did a nice job. Very nice. But I would have done it for you—you know that."

"Oh, no, no. I wanted to do it. Really. I needed something to do, now with Amy at school, and—"

"No dinner?"

"Dinner? Oh, I didn't realize what time it was. It just flew by today. I was so busy. So busy. I—I didn't know—"

Ray gave me one of his hugs. "Honey, what's wrong?"

"Nothing. Don't you like it? It's much brighter. And clean. Don't you—"

"No, something's wrong. Just tell me what it is."

I took a deep breath and fell into tears. "Where are the children? Don't let them see me."

"It's okay. They're upstairs."

"No, well. No. Ray, I have something to tell you. You have to believe me, because we shouldn't have any secrets between us. I don't want to keep any more secrets…"

Spots

In health class Mr. Plevnik once said that if a white person married a black person their children would have spots. Really. We had a good laugh about that in the locker room, but we had to be careful because Mr. Plevnik was also our gym teacher.

The only black people I met were on T.V. Most of them were stars. And some, like Pearl Bailey, seemed like members of my family. It was something about the way they were confident in their affection for everybody. Some members of my mother's family had dark skin— not that we had any African ancestors—but skin can be a lot of colors, and my grandfather's was the color of walnuts. He was Polish. I've noticed that Poles can be very fair, very dark, and very everything in between. Just like my family. I would see all these colors at funerals, reunions, and weddings.

Last year I went to college. I didn't go far—The University of Pittsburgh—but I was happy to be on my own, even if it meant living in a crowded dorm with a lousy roommate.

The door of our pie-shaped room opened up to a circular hallway, so it was pretty easy to get lost. I used the elevators and bathrooms for guidance at first, and then people started taping things to their doors, and that gave me a clue to where my room was.

I met all kinds of characters there, many from out of town, especially Philadelphia, our arch rival. They talked funny, almost like New Yorkers, but they also liked to laugh and horse around, which was something I was used to. There was this Jewish kid Marty with a great head of curly black hair, and another kid Bill from the hills somewhere who sounded like one of the Clampetts. There was a math and computer science kid named Jan whose room was filled with stacks of those connected sheets of computer printouts in a language called Fortran. His roommate, an overweight pimply guy, got drunk every weekend and played his electric violin very loudly to bands like the Electric Light Orchestra. At first it drove us nuts, then we kind of liked it.

Since I lived on the sixteenth floor, I spent a lot of time in the elevator. I met a lot of kids from the other floors there, such as girls, football players, our Resident Assistant (who looked the other way when we brought beer up to our floor), and a black girl who always smiled and asked me how I was doing.

If she ever caught me looking at her, she didn't let on. It so happened that our schedules must have been in sync, because we often found ourselves alone together in that elevator. She was interesting in many ways. There was something familiar about her, though I had never before had a conversation with a black person. It was in her jaw line, and the way she styled her hair (cheek length, neatly parted on the side, full). Her dark eyes intrigued me too, and the way her lips closed.

We met for most of the semester, and even had a little conversation or two. A few times some of her black girlfriends were in the elevator with us. Then she didn't look at me. And they didn't seem as interested in getting to know me. I felt out of place, thinking our little flirtation episodes were over.

I hung a few things on my small part of wall alongside my bed: drawings I had made, a calendar the school had given us, a card I liked, and a relief sculpture.

The sculpture was something I'd knocked off in my art class at high school. I wasn't too concerned with it, but the teacher really liked it and made me feel I'd made something worth showing off. So there it was on my wall: a mountainous form cast of plaster, then painted over in bright stripes that led on to an irregularly shaped piece of white plywood. If anyone asked what it was, I replied, "an organic form." That pretty much ended the conversation for most of the guys on my floor.

The sculpture, mounted on the plywood, was pretty heavy, so I hung it using the largest nail I could find for that little piece of wall. The only thing between me and the wall was a narrow shelf. I set a bunch of stuff there, like the hurricane glass I got when I was in New Orleans. One night at around 2 AM the nail gave, the sculpture landed on my face, and I jumped out of bed to step on a piece of my shattered hurricane glass.

This woke up my roommate, who thrashed around in his bed for a few moments before asking, "What happened?" A large building had recently exploded at the university because of a gas leak, killing two secretaries. A class of nearly three hundred had emptied out just minutes before it happened. So naturally we were all a bit on edge.

"My sculpture fell," I said.

"You okay?"

"Yeah, just got a cut on my foot."

He rolled over and went back to sleep. I found a bandage for my cut and swept up the glass. The sculpture had only minor dents in it, and I felt okay, so I went back to bed too.

At 7 AM my alarm rang, giving me a little jolt. I found my flip-flops, towel, and toothbrush and headed for the bathroom. I set them on the sink top, looked in the mirror, and saw I had a black eye—a nice half-moon underneath my right lower lid. It actually looked pretty neat, and was only slightly puffy. After my shower I proudly walked back to my room to show my roommate, but he was already gone.

My day was pretty unremarkable, and not many people said anything about my eye. After lunch I wanted to take a nap, and my foot was a little sore, so I got into the elevator of our A Tower and leaned back against its orange wall. Just before the doors closed my black friend popped in, holding a stack of books.

"Hi," she said.

"Hi." I couldn't think of anything to say. I noticed she scanned me quickly, looked ahead as the doors closed, then jerked her head back to me.

"What happened to you?"

"Me?" I had nearly forgotten about the eye. "Oh, nothing. Well, something I guess. I have this heavy relief sculpture hanging above my bed and in the middle of the night..."

Her hand went down.

"Right."

She laughed a little, the first time I'd heard her do that. "Oh, I'm sorry."

"No, no, It's okay. I'm fine. I have this killer black eye now."

She cocked her head a bit, and said *Hmm*. I wasn't sure whether she liked it or not. At that moment I pretty much decided I would ask her out, but her floor came and she left.

Mid-terms were approaching. My black eye healed. I got the flu, and spent many nights at the library with a pounding head. Everywhere I looked I saw chemistry problems. Anyone I met I engaged in Socratic dialogue. I forgot about the weather, about food, about girls. That is, until I saw her walking hand-in-hand with a guy who looked a little like Harry Belafonte.

It stopped me in my tracks. Now my heart pounded along with my head. She passed me by—I'm sure she saw me, but she never looked my way.

I forgot everything. Maybe I had been deluding myself. Maybe I was just some curious white boy who lived only in an elevator. I didn't even know her name. I found the nearest bench to sit down and think. I sat there a long time, even considered skipping my Russian class. But I ended up going to it, and not knowing anything when I was called on. By the end of the class I was less shocked, more focused, and ready to eat dinner. I decided to drop my books off in my room first, and wouldn't you know it, she got into the elevator right in front of me. She might have smiled, but I didn't look at her. She got off on the tenth floor, not her flour (the fourteenth). I was very proud of myself for being able to ignore her.

That evening I ate everything in sight, and went out late for a beer with some of my hall mates.

I came back at about 11:30, pretty drunk. We'd had one too many. We crowded into the elevator and headed up to our floor, but it stopped first on the tenth. We heard shouting on the other side of the doors. When they opened we saw her standing there, looking very angry. She barged right into the middle of us and slammed her hand on button 14. Then she folded her arms, took a deep breath, and waited. None of us spoke. Soon her floor came, and she was out.

Marty looked at me and shrugged. Someone giggled. In another few seconds the doors opened onto our floor. I made my way to my room and collapsed into bed.

I took my last midterm on Wednesday morning the following week, and felt as if I were walking on air afterward. It was a chilly day, but sunny. I stopped for a cup of coffee to take to my room. None of my friends, it seemed, were around in the lobby of our building. They were all off suffering their own mid-terms, I guessed.

The elevator, however, was a bit crowded with a lot of kids I didn't know. It was hard to be acquainted with the whole building, there were so many of us. I noticed her leaning against the back wall, her head down and hair covering part of her face. By the time we reached her floor most of the others were gone. She brushed by me on her way out and I mustered a bit of courage to say, "Hi." She turned to look at me, quickly, before hurrying out.

She had a black eye.

I mean, it was noticeably black and blue and yellowish, from her eyelid down to the skin beneath the eye. A real shiner. Was she an athlete? Had someone opened a door onto her? I was left alone in the elevator as it whizzed past my floor to the top, then began descending again. Maybe I should have said something, anything. But what?

When I finally reached my room I lay on my bed and stared at the ceiling. I was happy that mid-terms were over. I had a good cup of coffee to drink. I was attracted to a black girl. Had he hurt her? Should I run down to the fourteenth floor and save her? Did she even give a hoot about me? Would she tell me to get lost?

I thought of my family. We'd had arguments, contests of will, stubborn disagreements, and generally unpredictably chaotic encounters. But there was never physical harm. Never. How was such a thing possible? Since it was beyond me, it was probably best to forget it. She could take care of herself.

"Luke!"

Marty was banging on my door early the next morning.

"Luke! Come on, man!"

I was late. It wasn't normal for him to be waking me up. Usually it was the other way around. But neither of us wanted to miss our chemistry class.

While walking up the hill he brightened: "Hey, what about what happened in the tower basement?"

"What."

"You know, the murder."

"Murder? What tower?"

"Ours, stupid. You didn't know?"

"No. What happened?"

"They found the body of a girl in one of those big laundry bins down there. A black girl. Last night. It's all over the news. Where've you been?"

"Sleeping, remember?"

It took me a moment to register what he was saying. Then I froze. "What?"

"Nothing."

We kept walking.

Detached as I was, I feigned attention during class. It was not a difficult lesson, anyway. I sat in that room of nearly 200 and gazed at the backs of heads, the different colors and textures of hair, none of them belonging to blacks. It was as if those people didn't exist, or as if they existed, but only in certain compartments, certain times and places, all clearly defined. Deep down I felt as if I could have saved her. I could have at least talked to her, let her know that her situation could be changed. She had the power to do that. Why not? Didn't we all have the power to do that?

As I neared the dorm towers after class, I noticed now the police presence there. A couple of reporters caught students coming and going to ask them what they thought of the crime. Were they scared? Did they know the deceased very well? Was there ever an indication that violence was present on campus, something that might lead to this? Some of them answered in short phrases, others gushed at the opportunity to be on the news. Others just kept walking; I was one of those.

I walked up the steps to the lobby, feeling the weight of the world, something I couldn't shake off. I didn't want to speak to anyone. I nodded a quick hello or two to acquaintances, and headed for my room. I was hoping my roommate wouldn't be there. I wanted to be alone. I wanted to lie on my bed and stare at the ceiling, and think about how people are separated.

I did lie there, in a state of half-sleep, until I realized I should have some lunch. I rose too quickly; my heart was in my throat and I had to swallow deeply to dislodge it.

It was strangely quiet on my hall, hardly anyone around. I rode the elevator down by myself, by now wishing for company. I gazed ahead, as if in a trance, at the round buttons and their numbers. None were lit but the L for lobby. Then, slowly and quietly, the elevator stopped. I looked above the door. It had stopped on 14, her floor. I looked down, as if in respect, as the doors opened. A figure entered. The doors closed.

"Hi. My name's Cherie, by the way."

I looked up; her black eye was gone.

"I'm Luke."

III
OUT OF TIME

View

At the crest of a small hill, a hill that has not always been regarded in its long history, sits an heirloom building made of wood, two-story, long, low, with a front porch that spans the length of it. The building hovers over a commercial street, a busy street that leads in one direction to the outer suburbs, and in the other to more seasoned neighborhoods of the city. Most of the other buildings, in either direction, are of brick.

From this viewpoint, this hovering porch, patrons of the bar it holds may wander about in heated discussion, or laughter, or solitary despair. There is nothing this porch hasn't heard or seen, no conversation that doesn't echo another, no ghost that is unwelcome, though some of its ghosts go unnoticed—timid ghosts, like those who first traveled there from fear and longing long ago.

These were the slaves who hid in the building's cavernous basement, aided by a few local souls, who stole by night to points further north along the route of freedom. They wrapped themselves in fading quilts and slept by quiet streams in the heart of the Appalachians at the break of dawn, dreaming of Big Dippers and the dotted lights of northern towns. They traded their quilts with every conductor, and read the secret route that was handed to them in each new pattern. They brought a lifetime's store of memories with them as they lay in the basement of the solitary wooden house, some only in their teens, others not much older but broken into an early, deep maturity.

They roam, wrapped in their quilts, along the porch after midnight, after the house's newest guests have left, drunken, near-sighted, and oblivious to the past.

At two A.M., then, a boy walks by, a boy of fifteen on his way home from a soul-searching evening he has spent with his love, an evening of storm and calm set against the inescapable hum and life of a party. His heart has been opened, and everything he sees and feels pours in and out of it as he walks home in the cool, early-morning air.

She has started not to look at him when she speaks to him; her eyes, once two deep brown wells of mystery, are now tense and withdrawn, as if belonging to someone he has never known. He doesn't know what to make of it, or her, or his fifteen-year-old world. Everything has become for him uncertain, unclear, unpredictable.

In this limbo-like state he looks up at the house, its empty, wide porch, and notes that it is not empty. A lonely figure stands there, wrapped in an old blanket, looking either at him or past him—he couldn't tell which. Then another figure walks out of a shadow, looking in the same direction, and then another. Though it is night the boy can tell they are black men, all three of them; he has never seen a black man in this part of town before. He looks down, then, and keeps walking. But he cannot forget them.

The next day our tavern's owner, Bill Steeps, comes out at noon to sweep the porch of its first fall leaves. The broom, tattered and discolored, loses more of itself each time it is used. Bill wonders what he is sweeping away: leaves or stray broom. The last few nights' revelers have left beer stains on the porch's dusty floor. Bill stops and regards the floor, feeling its ancient weight and history, wondering if he will ever get it clean. He unexpectedly feels that he has never been able to keep it clean.

"Bill!" his wife calls through the open door. "Someone on the phone wants to talk to you. Get in here!"

Bill drops the broom to take the phone call. He knows he has been late paying his draft beer company, and has already rehearsed his excuse. Rita holds the phone up with her left hand, and uses the right to flip through a little notebook.

"No, no. I already know what they want," Bill says. "Here." He reaches out for the phone.

For the next ten minutes Rita moves about the bar, straightening chairs and re-organizing the counter, while Bill reassures the beer company. Then she steps outside for a breath of autumn air, and notices two cops making their way up to the porch.

"Hey guys. What's up?"

"Hey Rita," the thick-boned, sandy-haired one says. "Seen any suspicious activity on the street?"

"Like what?"

"Like a couple a black guys in a stolen Mercedes—gray—with a lot of cash to burn?"

"Bill!"

He appears on the porch.

"They're looking for a stolen car. Blacks."

"Never," Bill says.

"What's that?" says the cop.

"I said you'd never find them here. It's not usual, not since I've been alive anyway. I got nothing against them, but you know as well as I do—"

"We just got a report from Russ Kramer. They were in his store, bought two of his best audio systems with cash."

"Oh? When was that?"

"About two hours ago."

"Well we haven't seen them. Rita—right?"

She shakes her head and frowns. The cops nod, unfold their arms, and say they'll be by on Saturday night for a beer. Bill and Rita go back to their work.

It's a warm Saturday night for October, a freak of fall weather, bringing summer up again from the south, and sending more than the season's share of revelers to the tavern. They spill from the body-warmed room out to the porch, where the air is also still, but less used. Their voices carry evenly far into the night, up and down the busy street—commingling with the sounds of big engines, footsteps, and distant laughter—as if breaking through time.

Rita and Bill step outside too, leaving the night-work to hired help. There's not much that can go wrong on a night like this, with the lingering warm weather, the loyal clientele, and money in the drawer. Even that morning's argument has evaporated, leaving them both free to enjoy their accomplishments, their people, and each other.

"Bill—" Rita puts an arm around his thick waist. He tenses, then turns to her and feels relaxed.

"Yeah, hon."

"Bill and Cookie want us to go to Las Vegas with them next summer."

"That's a long way off. But why not? Sure. We've never been to Vegas. Hell, we deserve to go to Las Vegas!"

"Do you think we can afford it?"

"We can make sure we can afford it. This is America."

Bill feels a hand on his back. It belongs to his buddy, Ray, who speaks lowly into Bill's ear.

"I didn't know you were expanding the business to include other neighborhoods of the city."

Bill looks inquisitively at Ray, who nods in the direction of the bar. A small group of black Americans has just been served a round of drinks. They laugh and toast one another, unaware that they have been noted.

"I'm sure they're fine," Bill says. "I can't refuse business, can I?"

Ray's eyebrows rise, but he doesn't respond. A brief chill passes between them.

Our adolescent friend is walking with his love, walking again along the road that has been lonely for him more than once in his past. They are deeply involved in one another, the warm autumn breeze defining nothing but themselves, their worries, their situation, their love. It is approaching midnight, and they are nearing the tavern house. He has forgotten everything for the moment—all he can smell is her cherry-scented perfume; all he can see is the balance of pain and contentment in her eyes; all he can hear is her words:

"So what do you think we should do?"

He can almost feel her breath, though he is not looking at her.

"I don't know. What's wrong with the way things are?"

He takes her hand; she squeezes once and lets go. Then he looks up and sees them again, wrapped in their quilts, standing in the shadows at the far ends of the porch. They do not move, or speak, but he knows they are looking past the few remaining patrons, at him.

"Did you hear it?"

"What—" she freezes.

"They must be gun shots," he says.

"Oh my God. Where?"

He looks around, trying to locate where the sirens are coming from, to let himself slip back into the world. But before he can answer her, before he can let go of their insular life, he sees lights flashing far ahead. Sirens ring in all directions. Car doors slam; quick footsteps staccato the air.

They killed a black man, someone in the community said. And then another said it, and another. They all repeated these words: *They killed a black man.* The phrase went to sleep with everyone that night, and woke up with them in the morning. The phrase would not go away. It made the twelve o'clock news, and then the next morning's news, and the national news.

Bill and Rita started the day in each other's arms, something they had not done in a long time. Usually they started the day in confidence, already preparing their mental lists of things to be done. But this day brought an unfamiliar sense of caution to them: plans escaped them, and they ended up dreaming. It was the phone ringing that finally coaxed Bill out of bed. Rita allowed her empty embrace to linger, as she closed her eyes again and reascended to her dream-cloud, though Bill's words on the phone burned through:

"Yeah, Len. I don't know what—it happened so fast. Everything was gone from the drawer. Everything."

"It had to be—I guess—who else could it have been? I know just about everyone who comes in that place, you know."

"You're right, Len. What can we do?"

There was little left to say. Bill listened another minute to Len's tirade, then hung up, shaking his head.

"Well?" asked Rita, by now very awake.

"Well what."

"Was it *them?*"

"No one knows."

"Len seems to know."

"Len is being Len about this."

"He might be right."

"Look—what difference does it make? They were speeding and went through a red light."

"And they were carrying a lot of cash."

"All right, all right," he said.

She grew quiet. "Sorry, honey. Come back to bed."

"No, I can't. I'm up now."

"You're upset."

"Why should I be upset?" he shot back.

"I don't know. It's not your fault," she said.

"It's nobody's fault. Things happen. And we're out eight hundred bucks."

"That much?"

"Yes. Eight hundred thirty five." He stopped. "But how—"

"What?"

"How did they do it? Right under our noses."

"I don't know, Bill. It was pretty crowded that night. Talk to Doug."

"He doesn't remember anything. He says he just turned around and it was gone."

"Sounds like Doug. Are you sure he's not drinking back there again?"

"No. I'm not sure of anything with him."

Bill heard on the evening news that the man had died instantly. The police reported that he and the others had run the red light, appeared drunken, drove recklessly, and disregarded their pursuit, which ended in a car chase and warning shots. After coming to a halt in somebody's yard the driver stumbled out yelling vulgarities and reaching for something inside his coat. That is when they fired on him.

The reporter said that he had been reaching for a cell phone. The others in the car came out when called, cowering and whimpering. Together they were three young men and one woman. They said that they were not familiar with the neighborhood. They had been drinking, yes, but not locally. They had been invited to a late-night party in the area but had taken a few wrong turns.

This version of the story was new to Bill, who had relied on Len and a couple of other friends in the neighborhood to provide details of the incident. Ray was certain that they had been the ones in Bill's bar that night; he said he recognized the coat on the ground when he saw it on the news. He said Bill should call the police *right now* and let them know where they got the cash. Bill was mostly quiet; he felt as if he had been appointed judge against his will. After hanging up the phone Bill sat in his armchair watching television, whatever was on, whatever might draw his attention away from the incident.

On Monday night the bar was nearly empty. Bill kept the door open until eleven, then he told Doug to clean up and lock the drawer. Rita had already gone upstairs to bed; Bill spent the next hour rocking on the wide, empty porch. Monday nights on the porch were so still, it seemed, as if there had been no history but the history of stillness. The street was even quiet, offering only sporadic movement, the quick anonymity of occasional moving cars. No one was out walking that night; there was no wind.

Bill had been sitting on that porch for twenty years, and for twenty years that porch view had felt the same, withstanding renovations and alterations in the commercial scenery. Bill had come to feel, on late Monday nights, that he and that porch had a secret, a chunk of dedicated time that no one else knew. During this time he could step outside of Bill and see himself at another angle. It was an important time for Bill, and an important time for the ghosts.

Until now they had no reason for getting to know him—they saw him only as the latest occupant in their spiritual home, no less a product of contemporary culture than the others. What could they do with him? What difference could they possibly make? Their presence was sometimes noted, yes, but only by those who were willing and able to see beyond the limitations of their own narrow world and time. Until now, Bill did not belong to that small group.

As he sat rocking, making the only sound, a steady pattern of footsteps reached his ears. He looked up and saw a boy coming toward him.

"Hi Mister Steeps," the boy said.

"Hey. Aren't you Jake and Laurie's boy?"

"Yeah. I walk by here a lot."

"This hour?"

"My girlfriend lives down the road."

"What can I do for you, son?"

"Nothing. I was just wondering—I wanted to ask you—if it's true what they said on the news."

Bill stopped rocking. He looked the boy cold in the eye. "They were here, yes. And just after they left, the money was gone. Now I don't know if those officers were justified in what they did. But one thing I'll tell you: those blacks were criminals, pure and simple."

The boy looked puzzled.

"But they're regulars here, aren't they?"

"No, no, no. Never. At least not that I know of. And I know who comes to this place. I live here—" He pointed to the second story. "Everyone who comes to this bar is a guest in my house. My father lived here too, you know. This house has been in the family for generations. My honor and reputation are tied to this house—" He stopped, because the boy was looking off in another direction, not listening to him anymore. "What?" said Bill.

"Who are they then?" The boy turned his head toward the far end of the porch, where the ex-slaves stood under shadow, as still as the night, wearing quilts that were as translucent as October clouds over the Moon.

"Hey now!" Bill shouted. He looked around, caught a glimpse of them, then noticed they were gone. Was he seeing things? Had they been there all along with him, his private time violated, trespassers on his thoughts?

What if they were criminals too, avengers of those who had been caught? He jumped out of his seat and headed to the door. Once inside the bar, he flicked on the overhead lights. The money drawer was not fully closed! He had caught them this time. Should he call for help, yell, run after them? He made his way to the drawer, pulled it open and lost his breath. All of the stolen bills had been returned. Not one was even out of place.

The boy, left alone on the porch, backed down the steps. While heading home, carrying the weight of his full heart, he turned and saw them standing there again, this time waving, under a shimmering moonlight, until he waved back.

Superitsa

Superitsas live in the snow. You don't see them one by one, though—only vast numbers of them, glowing together on the hillsides on winter evenings and falling in through the cracks of the house to guide your dreams. They tell you things in those dream characters, characters who may seem familiar or unfamiliar to you, about choices you'll have to make, about your and your family's future, about the lives of strangers as well—as long as you have some connection with them.

Superitsas are there on summer evenings too, or at dawn in springtime, the day after your birthday, at weddings and funerals. Some may never know the Superitsas; some may go insane from knowing them too well. When I was alive I never feared them, but let them breathe into me. Now I am a Superitsa.

I was born in Croatia. The story I am about to tell you begins there, and ends in the hearts of my family: my Croatia across the sea. I moved there when I was fifteen, alone, on a boat crowded with hundreds of young men and women like myself.

A Superitsa does not always know what will come next, not any more than the living do. I had known Dajana's ancestors in Karlovac, before they moved to Tuzla, where Dajana met Bojan and they were married. Bojan was of mixed blood—Serbian and Montenegrin—but to Dajana he was a Yugoslav from Sarajevo, that enigmatic city where three worlds meet and bend around one another, sometimes peacefully, and sometimes not, but always elusively, like three snakes vying quietly for one striking pose. When the new war broke out they were newlyweds, and Dajana was expecting their first child. Seven months later Bojan was in Belgrade waiting for his wife to join him there; Dajana had had fled to Montenegro, where her baby was born two months premature.

This is nothing remarkable; young people from our land have always lived in the shadow of war. They may live the first twenty years of their lives only hearing stories of past wars, and then the next morning those stories come back to life: then they see nothing but animosity and hatred, distrust and contempt. And some of them learn quickly to hate, to carry on the tradition of a walking corpse.

Bojan would not learn. He watched many of his friends grow bitter, but he would not become bitter. When a favorite professor and mentor from the university advised him to leave, to abandon his birthplace and its history, to lose contact with his parents, to safeguard his wife and the child she was carrying, he took heed. But it was not easy.

Dajana had found passage before the city had been closed tighter than a fist. By the time Bojan had decided to join her—at his uncle's house in the mountains of Montenegro—the only way to leave Sarajevo was by falling in favor with the United Nations: not an easy thing to do. Thanks to Professor Radovic, however, it became easier.

Twice bullets came through the car windows; seven times they hit the body of the car. But Bojan was not hurt. After one week of ferrying messages between guard posts, under fire from Serbs on one side and Muslims on the other, Bojan was allowed safe passage to Belgrade, though not without the generous greasing of many palms. Soon afterwards Dajana joined him there with their new son, Dušan. Then Canada opened its doors.

I've always had a fondness for my oldest granddaughter, Ruth. She is smart and attractive, with strong blue eyes that hold a tight grip on anything she's talking about. She has seven children, little more than half the number I had, but she treats them fairly and wisely, with a sense of motherhood that I wasn't always able to hold. What I like

141

most about Ruth is that she meets me often, and uses what I have to tell her during her Earthly life. Why wait? It does no one good.

The season I am talking about here is winter, and Christmas just around the corner. Ruth was feeling even more giving than usual; a nice little snow storm was about to begin. Ruth has always liked storms—a thunderstorm at seaside being her favorite—but snow storms work almost as well for her. They let her see on the outside all the strong feelings she has on the inside. This little snow storm came over the northern hills and landed in her backyard. She watched the miniature white tornadoes swirl crystals about the yard. Joe was still asleep. She had the storm all to herself, not caring in the least that she might not make it to work that day—in fact, near jubilant at the very idea.

That's when she realized that this Christmas would be something different.

That day Bojan also rose early to make himself a strong cup of coffee, in the Turkish style. As he poured the finely-ground beans into a small pot he thought of his father, Stevan, who had always insisted on grinding the beans by hand with his ancient wooden grinder. Bojan's coffee would never be as good, though it wasn't at all bad. After the coffee and sugar rose to a froth in the boiling water he cut in more hot water, and poured himself a cup.

Out over Lake Ontario the sky hung low, gray and dishevelled, like unshorn sheep. Snow lay all about its shores: Bojan studied it all the way down the western side toward Hamilton. He wondered about Niagara, even further, and about the States in general. How were they different from Canada? Would there be more employment opportunities there? Would his baby have good medical care if they were to end up in the States? But maybe it was too much to think about. They were only beginning to know Canada, who had been so generous and kind to them. It would not be right to leave now.

And yet, he did not quite like this obligatory feeling he had toward this new country. It was not just his decision that they should come here: the decision had been thrust upon them; they had no choice.

So what could I do? I worked on his soul a bit, not directing it, but giving certain thoughts and feelings a door to open. He came up with the idea himself: he would call an American acquaintance he had met one summer in Czechoslovakia. Just to talk.

It was a six-hour drive up to Toronto from Pittsburgh. Luckily, the sky was clear all the way through the snow belt—from Mercer to Erie then Buffalo, and up around the lake to its northern shore. Luke spent most of the drive wondering what he could say to Bojan, just what to say to someone who's just come from hell.

He would spend two of their five vacation days back in Pittsburgh driving to and from Canada: twice alone through the sharp winter air; and twice with Bojan and his family, keeping conversation afloat as he brought them closer and closer to the United States, and my granddaughter's family. You see, Luke became family to me when he married Ruth's oldest daughter, Jean, who is as dear to me as her mother.

When Luke met Bojan that winter morning on the twenty-first floor of his government apartment building they hugged and smiled, and little Dušan looked up at them with joy and puzzlement. Dajana set to making coffee and lunch before they were to start driving the six hours back to Pittsburgh; she let Bojan and Luke sit together in the little sitting room, their attention given to the wide window, and all the world below it.

"I'm glad you called me," said Luke.

Bojan sipped his Turkish coffee and nodded quietly, pushing his tilting glasses back up his nose. His small black eyes smiled for a moment, then went blank:

"Yes. I decided to call to see how you are doing, but I am also glad that I am getting to see you." The eyes stopped on the coffee, and stayed there a long time. He went on:

"I don't know. I've been in Sarajevo and then Belgrade, then Hungary and now here in a short time. Now I will be going to the States also." He broke into a short laugh, like a hiccup, then lit a cigarette.

Luke did not bring up the war; he let Bojan find the topic on his own: He told the story of how he had decided to leave, how he had seen some of his closest friends become filled with the venomous hysteria and distrust that had been encouraged by certain leaders—

"Okay Luke, look. I am Serbian. I am not nationalist. I do not blame anyone for this. But I know that most of these atrocities you are seeing on T.V. are committed by Muslims. They will kill each other and say Serbs did it. This I know because the U.N. Commanders told me."

Luke listened with open eyes and an even mouth.

"And what about the Croatians?" he said.

"Okay." Bojan leaned forward to speak. His manner was always calm, even when he became more animated.

"Croatians are Catholic. They have always been with Germany, Austria-Hungary, et cetera. They have even the Vatican to support them. Muslims were Serbs until Turks came and forced many people to change to Muslim religion. And the ones with the most money could be saved, if they changed to Muslim religion. Now they have all Muslim countries behind them. And what about Serbs? They have nothing. They are mostly poor, and no one even helps them during wars, as in Second World War when Croatian Ustasi killed millions of them. Okay, Luke, I do not"—he emphasized this—"hate Croatians. My wife is Croatian from Tuzla. Problem is outside influence— Germany, United States, Britain. They want to make a decision to decide the future of my country as they always have..."

Now Luke saw emotion in Bojan's eyes; it replaced the resignation that had been there, though it did not last long.

"Anyway," he finished, "I don't care about them anymore. I just want my parents to get out of Sarajevo. I don't feel anything for that place anymore."

Dajana served lunch and they moved to the table. Her great black hair swirled loosely up to a clip at the back of her head. She was polite and relaxed, and Luke found her appealing, though something was lost in her dark eyes too.

They drove down from Toronto to Hamilton that afternoon, and then on to Buffalo, bypassing Niagara.

The United States did not feel much different to Bojan and Dajana, though Bojan remarked that the highway seemed to be in better condition than the one in Canada.

"We have some bad ones, too," Luke replied. "Wait until you see some of the streets in Pittsburgh."

"Pittsburgh, is it not so nice?"

"Nice? Well, it has character. It looks good from a distance, with the hills and bridges and rivers, and old houses close together going up the hillsides—but a lot of it is old, industrial-looking, run-down."

"Like Sarajevo."

"A little."

The snow was clear and bright south of the lakes, and during that part of the drive south they had used up most of their important conversation, and ended up daydreaming, as Dušan slept.

I was an only child, but I raised twelve of them. My granddaughter Ruth is raising seven, and she gave them all plain, beautiful names, the kind that never sound old or out of style: Timothy, Jean, Anne, Catherine, Peter, David, and John. They all have good, strong personalities; Ruth and Joe always draw a good crowd for their holiday parties, and the grown kids never fail to spice those parties up pretty well.

Now Annie, who comes after Jean, has blood that boils in our Balkan style. She is tall, like her sisters, and holds her head up sharply, like her wit. She is the only dark brunette among them: the rest are sandy blondes, as I was. Timothy, the oldest, is the only one who inherited his mother's interest in matters of philosophy and religion.

But I still love him. Now the youngest of the girls, Catherine, is a real beauty. And the other three—Peter, David, and John—would have caught any girl's eye in my village, if not with their looks, then by their endearing pranks and warm palms.

They arrived in trickles that Christmas season, now that all of them, even the youngest, had lives and places of their own. They met in the kitchen, hugged and slapped one another, traded jokes and fried pirogi. They stayed up late at night drinking beer and playing cards, and referred jokingly to their future Bosnian guests as "the refugees."

Luke pulled into the city late in the afternoon, Christmas Eve, with none of the snow around that he'd seen further north, and the temperature nearly sixty degrees. Pittsburgh gleamed, and Bojan (a civil engineer) remarked:

"But Luke, you said Pittsburgh was not so beautiful. I think you are wrong."

Luke said yes, he supposed it was; he hadn't considered the skyscrapers. Dajana said something in Serbo-Croatian, and Bojan, in his soft, determined voice, answered her. Dušan was up and looking around as curiously as his mother and father. Luke drove along the river on an old and narrow boulevard that was walled on the other side by solid rock, billboards, boxy row homes, and even a church—the one I was married in. The road was uneven and unpredictable, but filled with frantic drivers. Bojan kept a sharp eye on everything: the hills, the river; the cars and billboards and houses, as well as the people in them.

"Look at Dušan," he said. "He has already been in four countries: Yugoslavia, Hungary, Canada, and United States."

Dušan was the first to enter the house, as Luke held the door open and Dajana held him in her cupped arms.

Annie walked into the foyer from the kitchen—

"Oh! Lookey here! I didn't know—Hi, I'm Annie. You have a baby!"

Dajana tipped her head and smiled. Luke introduced her and Bojan to Annie and the others as they began to fill the room.

Dajana didn't talk much that Christmas Eve; her thoughts led her far away, and the comfort of being with an open, hospitable family made her remember her own even more. Jean and Luke decided to go to Midnight Mass, and asked the Yugoslavs to go with them. Luke only offered once, adding that he would understand if they preferred to forego the experience (neither of them having been raised with much religion). But they came along, and sat as diligently as if they had been to Mass every week their whole lives long. Only once did they feel out of place: during communion time. Dajana didn't quite know what to do; she and Bojan whispered a few things and they ended up laughing—Bojan for a few seconds, but Dajana for several minutes, uncontrollably, as if something inside her had let go, and was unsure of its direction.

The laughing came back at intervals the next day, during the annual Christmas party. It started with the immediate family during the Opening of the Gifts: Annie, the organizer of the bunch, had sewn together hand-puppets from scraps of cloth and felt, each one adorned with indelicate hints that pointed to that puppet's character in the family. A short descriptive list accompanied each puppet. Family members and their spouses took turns holding up puppets and reading from the folded strips of paper, while the others guessed who it was they were describing.

One of the younger boys' puppets had a retractable belly button and floppy, rabbit-like feet. Another was dressed as a priest (his childhood dream) and had legs that were longer than twice the length of his body. My granddaughter Ruth's was dressed as a cheerleader; some make-up had been applied very hastily around its very large button eyes. Luke's puppet had stubby legs and a long torso; one of the puppet's hands ended in a bunch of spaghetti (Luke is Italian). The other held carpenter's tools, and asbestos dust was sprinkled all over him: Luke and Jean had just bought an old house.

Bojan sat close to Dajana on a large armchair, and Dušan played on their laps. Their smiles told the others they could understand at least some of the family's inside humor; but still, they had little to say.

I stayed out of the picture that Christmas day, letting my family take care of them as I knew they would. What little snow there had been was melted; the air stayed cool and clear all day long, like the air from another season gone adrift through time, and bringing a blue sky with it.

The boys liked to stand on the back steps and smoke, get a beer, or welcome guests who had made it up the perilous driveway. One of the earliest guests to arrive was my daughter (Ruth's mother), who came with Ruth's sister, Caroline. I named my daughter Anna after my mother, but they all referred to her by now as Baba. Anna was my first, and she and I are not very much alike. But you understand that bond that is only shared with the first.

When she was introduced to the Yugoslavs, Anna tried to call up all the Croatian I had taught her. Bojan was nicely surprised, but Dajana was genuinely touched. The words Baba recalled she spoke perfectly, and Dajana helped her along, half-amazed at the old dialect coming from this thoroughly American grandmother's mouth. She gave Dajana a brief personal history, with the declaration that "We were poor, but we were happy."

Later, seated in the living room near the nine-foot Christmas tree, Dajana, Bojan, and Luke told Baba *their* story. Baba's eyes became knotted up, and she took Dajana's hand, shaking her head: "I'm so sorry, honey," she said, in English, feeling they understood.

From then Dajana relaxed a little, even having a bit of wine, and joining conversations when she only knew a word or two of English. And Dušan spent more time in the arms of others, feeling secure under the warmth of their timeless faces.

By late evening Bojan had ended up in the "smoking room," an area just off the kitchen that acted as rear entranceway and laundry room. He had been drinking beer all evening, as the others had, all men, including Jean's father and Luke. They stood telling stories, drinking their beer, and farting. Luke asked Jean's father, Joe, if he'd ever lighted one, as Luke and the others had in their adolescence. "Not yet," was Joe's terse reply, which brought the house down.

Bojan, his small black eyes now large with enthusiasm, shook in laughter. By now he'd drunk enough spirit to fill a kettle. His lips sparkled and his cheeks were flushed.

"This is exactly like Serbian party," he told Luke. "Just here, with the beer and the smoking room."

"And the farts?"

"Yes. Especially farts. Do you remember in Prague, when we shared a room with Ima, the Spanish girl?"

"What?" Luke didn't know where the conversation was leading.

"You were washing your face by the sink, and you farted. And you turned to me and said, 'Excuse me.' I knew then you are normal."

Luke smiled a little more and raised his glass:

"Živili," he said. And they drank.

Guests came and went, as they normally did at Ruth and Joe's Christmas party. But this year they seemed to linger. Was it the pure and clear air that filled their lungs with a new freshness, or appreciation? The family ties were strong that year; nearly everyone showed up, and then drinking a shot of *šlivovica* was mandatory. At certain hours they could barely make their way through the crowded rooms. And everyone was introduced on arrival to the foreign guests: Luke or Ruth or Jean sought them out, and the more people they met, the more Bojan and Dajana had to tell themselves they were not at home.

Don't tell me I'm not doing my job. There is always a lot of snow north of Pittsburgh in winter. As Luke took them back to Toronto that day after Christmas snow fell finely over the windshield, onto the slick road, and into the evergreen woods following them north back to Canada. And I caught Dajana's eye in the flakes; I held her very close and whispered to her: *here is your home, in memory, in your childhood hills of winter white and your mother's warm hand. I am your mother now, and I will carry your heart with mine and the hearts of all our ancestors; with Bojan's, and Dušan's, and Luke's; we'll all remember that we are home, no matter where in the world you find it—that wintered peace.*

Pravoslavie

The day was warm but overcast.

The priest began from behind the ikonostasis, his back to the congregation, singing:

Blessed be the Kingdom of the Father and of the Son and of the Holy Spirit, now and ever and unto ages of ages.

Laurie's aunt and the choir sang:

Amen.

Dark light spread near the six narrow windows on each side of the church; small vigil lights glowed above each ikon on the gilded screen that separated the church into two parts: the altar behind the screen, and the congregation before it.

Aunt Kush blessed herself three times—hurriedly, touching her forehead, heart, then shoulders right to left—with her thumb and first two fingers pressed together. Laurie did the same.

Laurie's Aunt Kush and Uncle John lived on Eighteenth Street in South Side, only a couple of blocks away from St. Vladimir's. Laurie's family had lived near them when she was a child. Now Laurie was staying at Aunt Kush's for a couple of days. She was helping her bake cookies for her granddaughter's wedding; she had always loved her great Aunt Kush's pastries. Uncle John was still asleep as she and Aunt Kush walked out the door to go to Mass.

The priest, his back still to the congregation, led their weekly petitions:

For the peace from above and the salvation of our souls, let us pray to the Lord. For the peace of the whole world, for the stability of the Holy Churches of God. For this Holy Temple. For our Archbishop.

He sung in Old Slavonic, the language of the Ukrainian Orthodox Church.

The choir answered him in low echoes and clear sopranos:

To Thee, O Lord.

Aunt Kush blessed herself three times again; Laurie had lost her place in the booklet she held: *The Divine Liturgy of Saint John Chrysostom.*

Everyone sat down. Laurie found her place again, and cleared her throat.

The red vigil lights flickered and softly lit the golden crown and robe of the ikon of the Mother of God: *Theotókos.* Medieval Slavonic words running along the ceiling above the gilded doors had the same glow; their glow came from the spreading shadowy light of the narrow windows.

The priest bent slightly and Laurie caught the gold in his vestments, the gold on the cross behind the altar with the painting of Christ crucified, the gold of the acolytes' scapulars. The rest was dulled red or blue, or browns.

The priest went on. Aunt Kush sat straight up, her legs crossed at their shins, hands folded on her lap. Her head titled slightly and her small eyes were still. Laurie's head moved around; she studied every ikon and design in the church. She studied her aunt's profile: the solid brownish skin, shadows under her deep-set eye, closed lips, curving thread-like folds leading down the cheek.

Aunt Kush bowed her head and her right hand flew up to her forehead again. The choir burst into slow prayer:

Glory to the Father and to the Son and to the Holy Spirit…

Laurie read the Slavonic text and tried to follow along, remembering a word here and there from her childhood, words Aunt Kush had taught her. *Pravoslavie*—True Glory, Orthodoxy.

Then Laurie smelled incense. The priest swung the incense boat out at the end of a golden chain; he swung it in every direction of the congregation, and in every direction behind the ikonostasis.

The light coming in through the windows grew and then darkened again. The red vigil candles stayed the same—flickering above each ikon and behind and above the distant altar. The acolytes came out holding long posts topped with white candles or ornate crosses. The priest soon followed with the Book of the Gospels.

The Mass went on; Laurie lost her place many times, but usually managed to catch up again. Aunt Kush never picked up a liturgy book.

Aunt Kush was the only Orthodox Christian in Laurie's family. When Laurie thought of Aunt Kush she thought of poker. Aunt Kush had always been a good poker player. When Laurie was growing up in South Side she liked to visit Aunt Kush and Uncle John. On Thursday nights Aunt Kush and her "ladyfriends" played poker. They called Kush "Chicken Eyes" in Ukrainian and drank ginger ale, sometimes with a little whiskey if it was one of their birthdays. As far as Laurie knew, the women still played.

Laurie remembered the nutbread: thin rolled bread filled with walnuts and raisins, like coffee cake. Aunt Kush always made this for the club to eat with their ginger ale.

One of Kush's friend's, Toots, booked numbers. Laurie had never asked why; she only knew that whenever a baby was born into the family they would play the following numbers: the baby's weight, the time of birth, and the month and day of birth. Toots won quite a few poker hands, but never as many as Aunt Kush.

Uncle John slept on the couch during these games, and Laurie sat at one end of the dining room or kitchen table with Aunt Kush. Sometimes the women spoke in Ukrainian, but Laurie knew after a while what they were talking about. For instance, so-and-so lost a baby, so-and-so was *different*, or so-and-so and so-and-so were getting a divorce. All through the card games a small red vigil light burned before the ikon of the *Theotókos,* Our Lady of Kiev, in one corner of the dining room beneath a small window which Aunt Kush never draped or opened.

Let us attend.

Wisdom.

Laurie looked up and saw the lector standing to the right of the priest, ready to read the Epistle.

The Epistle seemed both long and short; the reading was from Hebrews, 1:10–2:3. Laurie paid attention until the line: *Therefore we must pay closer attention to what we have heard, lest we drift away from it.*

Then her eyes drifted around the church again, up to the narrow windows near the ceiling and ahead to the lighted ikons.

Peace be to thee, who has read.

Alleluia, Alleluia, Alleluia.

The priest quietly said a prayer into a book. Then he sang: *Wisdom! Rise! Let us hear the Holy Gospel. Peace unto all.*

Everyone rose; they bowed their heads.

The reading from the Holy Gospel according to Saint Mark. Let us attend!

Glory to Thee, O Lord. Glory to Thee.

Along with the nutbread they sometimes ate poppyseed cake. Toots was a very heavy woman and sometimes, in the summer, her bra straps would be hanging down over her upper arms, which fell out of the wide arm holes of her pale shift dresses. Aunt Kush was almost as fat as Toots. The four or five women would finish half a poppyseed cake and at least one nutroll, along with the ginger ale with sometimes whiskey and coffee. Uncle John snored just under the baseball game on the television or radio. The chairs in the kitchen were yellow and sticky when they played in the kitchen, and the gray Formica-topped table was filled with little white specks. Laurie learned the game from Aunt Kush, and a few times, if it was a whiskey night, the women would let her play.

Blanche was the loudest of the ladyfriends, though they were all loud. Toots was loud when she won, or when she had figured out that somebody was cheating, but Blanche was always loud. Aunt Kush was only loud when she was accused of cheating, though Laurie knew that none of them every really cheated. Every now and then Uncle John grunted from the couch, which meant, "Quite down," but nobody paid attention to him.

Glory to Thee O Lord, Glory to Thee.

The Gospel was over.

The priest now walked back behind the ikonostasis, and came out again, this time holding the chalice and paten. He and the choir chanted to one another and then everybody sat down.

Aunt Kush usually won. Laurie liked to think that it was from her coaching. Toots always said she couldn't understand it, but she didn't care because she didn't need the extra money anyway. At the end of the night the women would take a cab home, or one of their husbands would drive down from the bar to pick them up. They didn't live very far. Laurie lived only three houses away; her parents usually let her stay until the end of the game. Aunt Kush would send Laurie off with a hunk of nutbread and a quarter if she stopped first at the ikon of the *Theotókos* and blessed herself in Ukrainian.

I believe in one God, Father Almighty, Maker of Heaven and Earth and of everything visible and invisible.

They were standing again.

They recited the Creed, and then the choir sang: *Holy, Holy, Holy, Lord of Sabaoth…*and the priest bent over the altar behind the doors and repeated the actions and words of Jesus at the Last Supper. After he had addressed the cup, saying: *Drink of it ye all: This is My Blood, of the New Testament, Which for you and for many is shed, unto remission of sins.*

The choir answered: *Amen.*

Then they all knelt, bowing their heads into their arms or hands. The priest continued praying to himself. Laurie looked over to Aunt Kush and saw a nest of gray hair; everyone's head in the church except Laurie's was down. Then a funny thing happened. A window blew open near the ceiling, above the ikons, and all the candles went out.

No one looked up.

An altar boy quietly left and Laurie's heart jumped. The church was not dark, but the ikons no longer glowed. The large red vigil lights behind the altar were out; the bread and wine were left unconsecrated.

Laurie sat back, then knelt again. She tapped her aunt's shoulder. Aunt Kush looked up and smiled, then tucked her head down again. The priest stood with his back to the congregation, still, waiting for the altar boy to return, as the bread and wine waited on the altar before him.

Laurie nearly stood up; she nearly ran out of the church. But how could she? Did she want to disturb them? Weren't they already disturbed?

The small window tapped the painted wall like a tickertape, making the only sound. The light outside was still dark, just barely enough for the church.

Sweat beaded above Laurie's upper lip; she coughed. She closed her eyes, but this only made it seem longer. It had been so long. Where had the altar boy gone? She checked her jacket pockets for matches; there were none. She didn't smoke. Why didn't she smoke? The small red vigil light above the *Theotókos* on the ikonostasis was out. The Virgin's skin was dark now; her face and her baby's face were flat, without eyes or nose or lips.

The altar boy returned with a long rod, bent at one end. He walked over to the space beneath the open window and reached up with the stick to close it. It made small sound: click, and was closed.

Then he lit the wick at the end of the rod, and began with the altar candles. People began raising their heads. The painted cross was bright again. He walked outside of the doors and began lighting the small candles, one by one, over the ikons of the doors. Some blew out and he had to go back to them. Laurie's stomach was tight; her breathing was quick. The Virgin's candle was last to be lit.

Aunt Kush raised her head.

The priest continued: *Thy Gifts, of what is Thine, we offer to Thee, in all we do for all Thy blessings.*

Laurie blessed herself three times—forehead, heart, and shoulders right to left, with her two fingers and thumb pressed together, in Ukrainian, and didn't look at Aunt Kush again until the Mass was over.

And Aunt Kush blessed herself again, along with the rest of the congregation, but Laurie only looked at the *Theotókos* ikon, watching its red vigil light flicker over the Virgin's face and hands.

· 1969 ·

November

Five-thirty and the furnace has just begun blowing. Ed is still asleep and will not be up very soon on a Saturday morning. There is time for morning prayers, said silently in the kitchen where she will not disturb him.

It is November: brown and rust leaves blowing in circles outside the window at the bottom of the back stairs. She has tied a housecoat around her full frame; her slippers feel like cotton around her feet. She doesn't look out the window, though she cannot help noting the gray air outside as she passes it on her way to the kitchen.

It is five-thirty-five and she flicks on the kitchen light. The light outside is growing, throwing leaves against her clean windowpane. The furnace throws warm air around her face as she sets the kettle on for tea.

Tea and toast with jelly. She prepares it and sits around the small kitchen table, watching her blue walls and the air growing brighter outside. She begins to pray.

Beginning over and over she cannot begin. Finishing the first line she cannot remember the second. Instead she turns to the window, to the leaves blowing there. The wind grows but the day becomes less bright. It is November the fifteenth in Pittsburgh, near the bottom of a long hilly street, a quiet Saturday morning in a city valley.

Five-forty-five. No lunch to pack for Ed; no children to send off to school. No grandchildren to peek at, no cartoons.

Our Father who art in heaven, *święć się Imię Twoje, przyjdź Królestwo Twoje, bądź wola Twoje, jako w niebie tak i na ziemi.*

The refrigerator begins: a loud buzz winding down to a hum. The furnace stops, ticking like cinders dropped down to a cavern.

Here comes little Bobby. With his big round Krupa face and her own Radziukinas eyes. He runs straight at her with arms out, straight at her and into her. She smiles, waits for him. And waits. Waits.

Steam rises from the stove. The tea is made, steeping before her and she continues to try to pray. She has said these prayers over and over every day for how many years? How many times has she examined, corrected, asked forgiveness for herself?

The tea is warm and burning her lips; the toast cools them and fills her mouth with sweetness, rest.

Now it's Celine up early and softly descending the stairs. *It's Celine with her black Russian eyes and delicate skin.* Celine, the sick one, the beautiful one, her own. Where did she get those eyes, Gen? And how is she, your Celine? She looks fine, don't you think? If she's made it to twenty-nine don't you think there's nothing to worry about?

Yes. Nothing.

It's a quarantine, Missus Krupa. Not even Ed can leave to go to work. It's scarlet fever, and we can't let it get out.

Yes, she understands. But food. Who will bring food?

Now it's Celine and she's coming to have tea and toast with her mother, smiling, good morning mum, and Genevieve waits with her eyes, waiting. Waiting.

The window has grown dark, flashing lighter gray then darker again. It looks as if it will rain. It is five-fifty-five.

Dear Mrs. Krupa,

You don't know me but I was a friend of your son Carl. My name is Paco and I come from New Mexico.

He always talked about you and his brother and his father and sisters. He would tell me the same stories over and over. He was very fond of his family, and proud of them.

I'm sorry to have to be the one to write you this letter. But we made a pact together before leaving that if something happened to one of us the other would write the family. Your son was a good soldier and a good friend. It was very painless the way he died. A shell exploded into our ditch and he didn't feel anything. We have been good friends for a long time and I was proud to know your son. And he was very proud of you.

It's a war-sky outside her window, though she has never seen a war.

Genevieve is sixty-eight. She has twelve grandchildren. She thinks of them: none look like Carl or Celine or Bobby or the others who have left. The grandchildren are another life; the older life has left. But why so quickly. She must pray. To think about it is praying. She is waiting.

Give us this day our daily bread, *i odpuść nam nasze winy jako i my odpuszczamy naszym winowajcom.*

Six o'clock.

Still morning and the house as quiet as a nail. The furnace begins again; the kitchen is warm. It is a room full of children, busy aunts and uncles, Genevieve's mother, and Ed.

There are pots on the stove, one full of noodles. The other duck soup. Busia is slicing the cucumbers; the children are fingering the noodle dough. Genevieve thinks: marjoram and peppercorns, noodles twenty minutes, Busia wants coffee, Celine needs medicine, Laurie clean the floor, Adam shovel coal, Ed's listening to the news with his father.

She is pregnant. Number twelve. Another miscarriage? A Krupa? A Radziukinas? Solarczyk? Gołębiewski? What saints' names are left? Will she know this time, feel it die inside her, know that she has killed it with her work?

Mum, make taffy. Can Busia help?

Mum, I'm *bleeding.*

Genevieve, the water's boiling.

How about a beer, Gen.

The soup is too thick.

The stove needs cleaned.

Snow tonight. Father Rokosz says snow.

A ty mały djabeł!

It's Leo and Clara. Hi Uncle Leo. Hi Aunt Clara. The *czarnina's* cooking. Busia says it's thick.

It is *not thick.*

It is snowing. The window flickers evenly now, battling the kitchen light. Genevieve pours herself more tea, slowly turns and seats herself at her shiny table. The kitchen is in order; only she knows the order. Only she knows every square inch of this kitchen, as if it were part of herself, something she has seen every morning for how many years? As if it were her child.

How many children do you have Missus Krupa?

Well, three.

Oh, I heard you had about nine. Must've heard wrong.

Well, no. I did have nine. But they're not all here anymore. There was Carl killed in the war you know, and Celine, who left us, and the rest, well. I'm just waiting for my grandchildren now.

Now the twins are crying, the twins two weeks old. *Lying so close in the tiny crib.* Who is prepared for twins? She is filled with wonder, though she tells everyone how much work they will be. She is thinking of how they will grow up, play together, how different, how wonderful it must be. And then they stop crying. They are not satisfied or sleepy or happy, they just stop crying and the air waits for her to go over and check the crib. But Genevieve waits too, waits for the correct feeling to grip her, waits for patience and strength to come back. She is waiting.

The snow on the windowsill is one-half inch thick. It is six-ten. The refrigerator stops humming, and the furnace ticks slowly before beginning again.

She rises and walks to her sink, stands there looking at the window. The kitchen is so warm and the snow is falling fast. But Genevieve doesn't really think about it: she sees the snow, but doesn't think about it. She thinks instead of the window, of when she will clean the window.

Six-fifteen.

How many times must it happen, Father?

Remember, it's your duty.

It's my duty and I accept it, I accept it for God and for my family. Even if my babies must die. I will wait for another one. Another one.

Remember the Holy Spirit in your prayers and pray to our Blessed Mother for strength.

It's strength I pray for Father, yes, every morning and every night. I know one day I will have it. When my babies are born and grow up so I can see them and know that they are here.

The Lord be with you.

And with your spirit.

It is almost six-thirty and though Ed will still be sleeping there is work to be done. There is the morning, empty as a shell, and there is the day and the evening.

Ed will wake and there will be breakfast. Clara for tonight's card game. There will be laughing and forgetting and eating and talking.

I'm waiting for you, Celine.

She walks from one window to another, checking the panes for smudges.

And here comes Carl to fire up the furnace. Adam will you help him. Bobby, stay out of their way.

What color is the sky. Where did it come from, the snow. How long will it fall and how much. It is a nice snow for November, though no one is ready for it. Genevieve is not ready for it. It fills up their gravel driveway and settles on their window ledges. It stalls buses and trips you during your Saturday shopping. The card game may even be canceled tonight.

It is six-thirty, time to work. It is six-thirty and November, the first snowfall. Morning has begun, sleep is over. Dreams are over. The past is over, memory over. But it is six-thirty, time to begin. Ed is asleep. And Genevieve is waiting.

Eva

July 23, 1902
Posen (Poznań), Prussia

Strange voices, strange words I do not know. Mamusia holding me tight so I cannot breathe. But she smells the same to me. Why is she worried? We are going on a long, long trip, she tells me. How do I know we are never coming back? There are too many others going on this trip. I can smell them. She gives me something to hold: something soft at the top and long at the bottom. I hold it up to my nose. It is a flower, but there is nothing to smell.

August 4, 1904
South Side (Pittsburgh)

It was hot then, in the middle of the night. The window was open and footsteps clicked along forever in one direction, never disappearing, never, until I fell asleep.

January 14, 1907
South Side

Mamusia went to heaven. I sit alone now. Aunt Genevieve will take care of me. Her hands are not as soft as my mother's, but they know a lot. They touch my shoulders as the priest says his funny words. Afterwards we have a lot to eat. Everybody smells good. I think I can smell my mother, so maybe it's true what Aunt Gen tells me—that Mamusia is not really gone. I hear a lot of voices, but not Mamusia's.

May 11, 1908
South Side

Aunt Gen took me to visit a special school, the school for people like me whose eyes don't work. We walked a very long time and her hand was hurting mine but I didn't say anything. Aunt Gen has been talking the other way with me lately, the way I hear others on the street talking. She says they speak that way in the special school and I will have to speak that way when I am there. I think I can do it because I love Aunt Gen. The sun is setting right on top of my head and feels good. Sweet winds fall all over me; I know the flowers are blooming and it makes my heart jump. Will the special school smell as good?

October 23, 1911
South Side

I can use my cane to walk down to the corner, where Mr. Feldman meets me and walks with me to school. The horses pass by; I listen to the conversations in their carriages as they fade away, until another one comes. Mr. Feldman doesn't hold my hand. He doesn't speak, but I know he is there; I know his walk and the soap he uses.

March 14, 1913
South Side

I'm walking one day and stop to feel the sun. It has been a long winter. School is not as interesting as it once was. Everything is changing for me. I don't want Aunt Gen to get my dinner; I want to get it for myself. I want to just sit here and think, to remember my mother and be mad at her for dying. I want to skip my lesson tonight. I want to go away, just to see what happens.

While I am sitting on the low wall a ball bounces up to my leg, a hard ball. A boy comes running after it and asks me to throw it back to him. I feel around but it is gone. He calls me a stupid invalid and fades away, just like everything in my life fades away. I can't keep anything near me; I have no control. I have nothing. I feel the wind raising every hair on my arms. The air becomes chilly. My heart races. I get up, and go home to Aunt Gen. She will not know what I've been thinking about, but her hands will know.

What do other hands feel like, a man's hands?

July 4, 1915
Geneva (on Lake Erie), Ohio

I put my feet into the lake, one at a time. I read the pebbles with my toes, trying to make sense of them before I realize that God put them there just to be there, and not for me to read. Mr. Feldman did not come on this trip; nor did Aunt Gen. Miss Howe is here, and Sebastian, and Mary and Syl. Mary talks a lot; I don't want to talk these days—there is a lot for me to think about. There is blood coming from me; I feel that I can't keep clean. I go into the water to wash it away. The water is gentle and strong. I call for Miss Howe.

December 5, 1917
South Side

My feet are aching from the cold. I told them I didn't need help to walk, but now I wonder if I will make it home. Sometimes I slide; the cold bites into my face.

I pass the door that stays open during the summer; today it is closed. Just as I am passing by a man brushes by me. Come in, he says, I'll give you a warm drink. No, I say, I shouldn't do that. Suit yourself, slip and fall, lie out here in the cold. There are a lot of people getting warmed up in the saloon, he says. I nod, and walk in his direction. The door is open; a sweet smell comes out of it.

The inside of a saloon is not what I'd imagined it to be, not what Miss Howe and others say about them. It is not quiet, but full of talk. People are not miserable, but bright and happy. That man, his name is

Cal, gives me hot tea with something burning in it. It's bitter and hard to drink, but it makes me warm from the inside out. A woman named Pearl puts her arm around me; she is wearing a perfume made of roses. My toes are no longer cold; I can start to feel them again. Everything seems easier: talking, laughing, being alive seems easier. I stay there for a long time. Pearl takes me home. She says it is late. How late, I ask. Just late. The air is not as cold; I am warm from the inside, so warm I loosen my scarf.

September 19, 1923
Oakland (Pittsburgh)

Little John called me pretty today at school. Why did he call me pretty? I wander around town after teaching. I wonder who will see me, what they think about me. If they think I am pretty.

March 7, 1924
St. Joseph's Hospital, South Side

They say there is a baby in me. A baby growing. I try to feel it, but I can't. They say that it is why I am so tired, why I fell and knocked my head on the steps. When I breathe in, I feel the air move deeply inside me; it is a happy feeling. Why is no one else happy when they come to see me? Sister James William comes by and puts her cold hand on my face and whispers Poor Dear. Dr. Skrabski comes by with two other sets of feet; they mumble and then he speaks too loudly to me to tell me I'll be fine, don't worry. But I don't worry. I just feel light inside, emptied, I guess to make room for the baby.

The night before I go home I have a dream. That man is coming near me again, breathing loudly, telling me I am pretty. My legs are cold and he presses against me. I try to think, they told me to stop and think, but I can't. I can't think and I can't talk, until he is finished. Then I say—*No.* He laughs. Someone else is coming, and he tears away from me. I hear him running. I say again—*No.*

August 29, 1924
Oakland

Little John asked me why I have to go; he likes when I read to him. He wants to learn to read the way I do. All the children are asking why, and I am wondering how I will explain it, but then Miss Christian, the director, comes in and tells them I am ill, I must go and recover, I'll be okay, she says, but I must go.

I tell Miss Christian I am not ill after the children leave. I wait for her response; there is none. She shakes my hand as if she were at a receiving line—quickly and softly—as if she didn't know me. I understand a lot of things now about people. I feel proud and then sad and then proud again.

At home I hear Aunt Gen and Uncle Ed arguing about me, about where I should go, what I should do. Now I understand this too: I am a burden to them.

April 5, 1934
Chicago

Sister Rosamund has died. I sit in the funeral parlor, drenched in tears and thick floral scents. I remember the flowers that came to my hospital room when I had my baby. They let me hold him once. I try to forget the feeling, but it never goes away. It's a feeling that makes me want to live, so that I might feel it again—a feeling that is somehow connected to Sister Rosamund dying. I was her child, and she was my mother. She taught me how to give more, so that I could lose my grieving. Now I am afraid again. I haven't been afraid for so long because I have been a part of the convent for so long. There is no fear here, only giving. I have been giving for so long, giving out food, comforting so many others, that I have forgotten who I am. I am lost; my mother has died again. I am empty, and I don't know what will fill me.

October 30, 1935
Chicago

Children come by for candy, and I put it in their palms, like handing out the last parts of me, before I go West. Already it is cold. They say it is warmer there, and that I am needed there. I am *needed.*

How do *I* need?

February 12, 1936
Sacramento

I go to sleep smelling of bread and soup. I smell the old, unwashed clothes and manure on the boots of migrant workers. I smell eucalyptus after rain, and I hear strange accents on the lips of children. I know they are looking at me. They are wondering why I am here. I am losing myself in work. I feel invisible; just as the world is invisible for me. Maybe I don't exist. I have never existed. I fold invisible clothes with my invisible hands; I hand out pockets of air called bread. Invisible people say thank you with their invisible mouths. I am alone on a street corner in Chicago, cold and invisible. The wind rushes by from a monstrous, invisible lake and pushes me along to nothing. I walk in the nothing until someone touches my arm. I cannot speak. A baby slowly fills invisible parts of me. I know it will someday not be invisible. But not to me.

April 13, 1937
Sacramento

I open the window and know it is April, because the almond blossoms come to me on the wind. Now I forget everything about my life; I stand by the open window and let the scent fall over me, like incense. I am at church—my own church. Nothing can harm me.

May 7, 1938
Sacramento

The first wave of heat feels good resting on my head and shoulders as we walk from the convent to the kitchen.

I am standing at the doorway, welcoming people. A man asks me how he can volunteer; he has a voice unlike any I've ever heard, a calm voice, gentle and strong. Throughout the morning I hear him in the background, above the others. I feel a little chill on the back of my neck when I hear that voice.

I walk home thinking of nothing else.

July 20, 1940
San Francisco

The ocean is like a terrifying rain that comes up from the ground. It swells unpredictably, pulling me in too many directions. Jack holds my hand; then I can laugh. I feel so much of Jack in his strong hand, so much of his gentleness. So much of my world is now Jack.

October 13, 1940
Monterey

I can tell by the night-sounds that dawn is near. Jack is asleep, his great body heaving with life. Night is no longer cold and dead for me; it is the warmest part of my day. Jack is my husband and he loves me more than air. I am inside his breathing body, filling him up with something neither of us can see. Something, he tells me, like air.

June 27, 1941
Monterey

I stop. I think—what day is it? What season, year? How long have I been here; have I ever been anywhere else? I have never been in need, never felt unneeded or unloved. The sea's wind has cleaned it all out of me. I feel forever. Jack's arms are the arms of the world. My hand follows the curves of his face. Everything my hand has ever felt is in his face. I want to give back what has been given to me. I want to unlock everything that has been locked away in me, that needs to find a voice, a way out of my overflowing heart. Wait, Jack says, I will find a way for you to do it. What, I say. A few days later he says: you can go to college.

February 1, 1942
Monterey

I know silence. I know what it means, the different kinds of silence. This silence is one that frightens me: it seems that it will go on forever. I walk quietly so I will hear his footsteps coming; they do not come. I feel the walls closing in on me. For the first time I can remember I scream; then I talk to myself, I laugh. Footsteps come. They are not his.

Who will take care of me?

November 2, 1942
Monterey

I hear Jack under water, calling me, calling me. I smell him next to me when I awaken. I feel him brush against me as I prepare dinner.

I hear them whispering behind me on my way to the market, but their whispers fade to Jack's voice. I sit on the pier where Jack's boat was moored, and listen to the waves lap against the piles, telling little stories about Jack, about us. More and more I feel no need to talk.

August 11, 1944
Monterey

I close my eyes in the dark. It makes no difference.

October 1, 1944
San Francisco

A hospital again. I am lying down, listening. Listening to my breathing, listening for a long time. Then I feel there is something in my arm. I haven't spoken. My mouth will not let me. I can smell the hospital. There is no one else in the room. I can go to sleep again, just sleep. I can sleep without words, without anyone else.

November 19, 1944
San Francisco

I sit in a room, and they talk to me. I remember hearing other voices; I can connect voices sometimes. Other times I cannot. They bring me something different to eat; they tell me how it is different and that I will like it. But I cannot taste it. I eat until I can't remember why I'm eating, why I'm sitting here, why they are talking to me.

I walk with someone's hand holding my hand. I am not holding it back.

February 6, 1945
San Francisco

I feel warm by the window. The air comes clean to me; the sun comes clean. I get up and walk. I ask to leave, to study how the sun makes me warm, how it makes me forget.

April 1, 1946
San Francisco

Cells are little pockets of light. I am made of them. Each one has a universe inside it.

October 12, 1949
San Francisco

Dear Aunt Jen,

You must forgive me for running away. I have a lot to explain someday to you. But for now I want you to know that I always think of you and what you did for me. I will be taking my degree at the university here next spring. Unlocking my mind has also unlocked my heart. I love you, Aunt Jen. Please don't think ill of me. I am doing very well here. The university is a wonderful place. I feel my whole life has led me here, and that I will never feel out of place again.

May 11, 1950
San Francisco

I know my students by voice. I feel their worlds, each the same as, but a little different from, mine. I know what they are feeling; I know what they will be discovering. I am their mother, and I will not leave them.

August 5, 1950
San Francisco

I am a mother. Though I share this motherhood with many children, there is one who belongs to no one but me, one who has grown up not knowing the mother who carried him. A baby. My boy. A bloody birth scent. I haven't smelled it anywhere else, yet I wake up with it every morning. Then it disappears. Twice disappeared. A thousand, ten thousand times—disappearing.

November 19, 1952
San Francisco

My heart is in my throat when I awaken, when I realize that much of my life is over. I realize too that there must be much more; that I have been emptied, then full, many times—a cycle that will be repeated, but how, for how long?

Maybe I will do the filling: I will find the missing parts of my heart.

March 12, 1953
Train to Chicago

I hear them talking about the landscape—how severe, how beautiful it is. How it keeps changing. They say it is like traveling on another planet. A boy keeps asking his mother: how long, how long. I read poetry with my hands. The boy asks his mother what I'm doing. She says I don't know.

March 14, 1953
Chicago

I feel that wind again. It stops me cold. I stop and cannot think. Someone touches my arm and I shrink. Do you need a cab, ma'am? Yes, thank you. The Sisters of Mercy convent on, on— . I know where it is, what's left of it. They moved, you know, after the fire. Only a few of 'em survived.

The wind creeps into me. I freeze with fear. The cab driver has nothing more to say.

March 22, 1953
Chicago (The Convent)

They say they have found him. I hear mumbling through the walls, night prayers. I try to say mine, but they are replaced by fear, longing, anxiety, anger, and compassion. He is twenty-nine-years old. He will have nothing to say to me, but I must take care of him. I run my fingers slowly over my face, the way I did when I was a child. I run them over his face.

June 3, 1958
Chicago

I hear the door close again. It is too much for him. He doesn't come back for days—back in his old life and I back in mine. When he returns he brings a woman. She is quiet near me, but he takes my hand and brings it up to her face; then I know this is permanent, that I must bless the permanence. He asks about Jack. I don't answer him. I am not answering myself. I cry in my room, but feel there are no walls around me.

November 2, 1958
Chicago

The warm days are a memory again. The walks I took with Jay. The day I met his foster parents. His voice as he explained who I was—the pauses he made, and the way he finished a sentence. I felt at home in that voice. Wherever I heard his voice, I was home.

Now winter is coming back. I wonder how long I will live alone again—no Jack, no Jay and his wife, no Aunt Jen and Uncle Ed, no Sister Rosamund.

Jay floats around me: in, then out of my life. He is proud and, I can tell, a little angry—with me?

May 17, 1959
Pittsburgh

Such commotion. Everything so tight, so fitted together. I feel the curve of hills about me, how they tuck me in again. I sense Mr. Feldman's ghost at the school, his hand guiding mine; his lips forming his perfect words again. They are comforting words, telling me I have done well, that he appreciates the work I am carrying on. From my room I hear the cars on the street, the voices of people not connected to the school. All around me now are voices, all day.

April 20, 1965
Pittsburgh

Her voice spoke to me, a voice that came through all the others, drowning them out with her soft, sweet words. She talks about her new house, the big yard it has, the cat that lives next door. I hold the phone so close, it hurts my ear. She tells me all she sees: the way the big tree reaches up, the blue and white of her room, her dolls lined up on the second shelf. It is a life I never lived, but one I am living. I feel no difference between my life and hers.

February 9, 1968
Pittsburgh

I knew the footsteps; I opened the door before he could knock. He was alone.

He put my hand to his face, and I could feel he had aged. Why did you come without telling me, I asked. I was passing through town, Amy wanted me to give you this. She says she wants you to visit us. Do you, I said. You can come any time, but I might not be there. He puts the rough piece of paper in my hand; I feel the waxy spots where crayon was added. He puts his hand on my cheek, and presses it. He is pressing my flesh to my flesh, himself to himself. I love you, he says.

August 4, 1970
Pittsburgh

Amy and her mother asleep in the other room. I awaken in my familiar timeless stare. I dream awake; I dream of Jack playing with her, of our family. I listen to her tell me about the things she is discovering, and ask her to describe the coin I hold, the sun I feel, the way the wind moves things. I move freely when Jack is there; I don't worry about losing her.

Jack is moving underwater, softly rocking back and forth in the dark nothingness. The same nothingness. He is here.

June 18, 1975
Pittsburgh

My old hands turn the pages, my stiff fingers run over the braille. I have Proust, Thoreau, Dickinson, Steinbeck, Dostoyevsky, Welty, Frost. How long will I live? I am consumed by my books, by their descriptions of this world. I will imagine every inch of it, alone. There is little else left for me to do. As my body slows down, my mind speeds up. I am being led somewhere. I could sit and read forever. Forever is what I've been seeing all my life: a blankness infused with my thoughts. Nothing else. To know the world I must work—I am used to this kind of work.

July 22, 1978
Pittsburgh

Yes and no. Here and gone. Alive and dead. My blood is alive in her, but my Jay is dead. She called to tell me: her sweet voice now become a complex adult voice, with every history of emotion in it, everything her senses can bring to it. That voice, with its tragedy and girlish honesty, calms my heart. Life is beginning to make no sense to me— whom it chooses, whom it lets go. Whom it lets go part-way, or only gives itself to partially.

I loved him.

January 3, 1981
Pittsburgh

I don't care where I am now. It is a kind of freedom.

September 27, 1983
Pittsburgh (Nursing Home)

The doctors come and go, always surprised that I catch everything they're saying. They're holding something back, though. They put their hands on my face and pull my eyelids up, to look into my nothingness.

176

They see something there. Do I want my life to change, they say. I think, why, what is there left to change.

There's no guarantee, but they say it could change everything for me. Would I want them to try it. Next Tuesday.

They leave and I am left to think. But nothing comes. Everything I've read—all the descriptions of this world—leave my world a blank.

October 3, 1983
Pittsburgh (Eye and Ear Hospital)

Eva?

Yes.

Tell me what you see.

I see hell. It's frightening—pieces moving, feelings colliding, places behind my back, behind my head, which deceive me.

Why do they deceive you?

Because everything was equal to me. Now it is all set up for me to judge, to pick and choose—should I look here, or there? Do I think only about what I'm seeing? How can I still think, while I'm seeing?"

You'll get used to it. Close your eyes now. Rest.

April 5, 1984
Pittsburgh

Something is happening. I feel I no longer inhabit this world. I am some place else. I connect the world I know with the one I'm discovering, and they don't always match.

September 10, 1984
Pittsburgh

The children who cannot see come up to me, take my hand the way I used to take theirs. I see now how they read the world, the gift of seeing in a different way. Thank you, they tell me, as they've been instructed to say. Everyone is thanking me, naming a hall after me, helping me up and down the stairs. The school I knew moves with me through the rooms, tapping me on the shoulder: Don't forget about me.

November 15, 1984
Pittsburgh (park by the river)

The old season comes. I grab a dangling blue flower from one of the garden beds. I hold it lightly and let my fingers describe it. It feels familiar—I throw it out to the water. This is for you, Mamusia. There are no photographs of you, and none of Jack. I see you still in the old way, the way I'll come to you. The old light that was mine. The place that came before, that made me love what now I see.

Paradise.

These Words

To me, all light is blue. I can not even say it is shades of blue, though it flickers, changing shadow, darkness with little blasts of light.

I sit in a corner, always. To my back there is, as far as I can tell, nothing. But my view can change, and always does. It seems I can not control it, though everything before me is in my thoughts, thoughts that have a life of their own, even if they are tied to memory.

I had a family once, two little faces that came from me and a loving wife. They pass in front of me, inquisitive, playful, mindful of living. I see them differently now. I no longer yearn for them, nor do I wish to ignore them. I have all the time now that ever was. I will not control their fates.

I hover about to stroke them. I am never tired or hungry. It seems they may still know me, but I am aware of what divides us. I also know that we will leave one another again; afterwards I will never see them so close, and anything I can do now will follow them for as long as they live.

My death came rather suddenly. I had no time to prepare for it. Instead, I went blank, feeling nothing really. It was the first time I'd felt that way, not in control. Lonely. I couldn't be concerned with myself. I went into the operation with a beating heart—I remember feeling it, wondering how it would feel when I woke up. I didn't know I would be waking up in a new way, separated from hunger and the touch of my wife's hand. I couldn't feel other things, too. Emotions seemed distant, and worries. It seemed that they had been tied to my perceptions of them. They were relative. Now nothing is relative, only absolute. One thing does pain me though. That is the ability to see through time, and know that my wife and children will have to live in a world where everything is relative. They will compare the state I'm in only to things they've heard, or read, or been instructed to believe. And none of it will matter, because none of it is true. They will not know that I am existing in a state of nothing, the nothing that is left after you have peeled away everything you once thought mattered.

Not having to eat, or sleep, or worry about the state of a body does not mean I have nothing to do. I am aware that I must exert myself in one more way before I make the final departure. And in my world of absolutes there is no room to fail.

Here is what I must do: I must give those I've left a glimpse of the absolute. But I have received no instruction how to do it. I believe this is the same for everybody. When I approach others, others whom I know exist near me, they flee. My ancestors too have remained elusive; they have made the leap.

So I am on my own. I insist that it is not a sorry state. I am up to the task; there is no choice here. You summon a will you had never thought possible.

I must explain however that I am still locked in to the world I left behind. I understand that this will not always be. Upon completion of my task, I will dissipate. Those I once loved will then carry the burden I now carry. They too will be expected to pass it on.

It began with my wife. I found her at dawn, the window open and filling the room with a chill. She turned on her side and I felt I could still be with her, that I might wrap around her to protect her from the things I would not be able to see in her future. But the present was what concerned me. I could sense the things she had planned for the day. I could also sense that she might not do any of them, but walk about the house all day instead, tending the children, as if she had given up on herself.

She rose to close the window, and folded her arms around herself to keep warm. She didn't know I was part of the that chill.

I could feel every step of hers: the weight, the familiar weight of supporting a mortal body. It was almost crushing. She lifted a hand to pour milk, and I could feel that hand too. Every movement of hers was studied and painful, as if she were learning everything for the first time. The lines of her face were all flat and level with the earth— nothing pointing up or down.

It was then that I touched her, lightly, in a way I had not touched her before. She stopped, sat down, and breathed deeply. Earth lost its grip on her, and she forgot its weight for a moment. That was all I had to do.

It was Laurie's sense of adventure that had drawn me to her from the beginning. She was not afraid to leave the comfort of the neighborhood she had grown up in, to travel across town to mine, where she found work. I watched her as a pharmacist apprentice, the way she moved about our store, the sparks that flew from her in my direction. Yet I could see that she was also a bit shy—a strange and attractive combination.

As I touched her that morning I wanted to re-awaken that determined spirit of hers, the one that would allow her to survive. I followed her for days, hovering near her shoulders. Often she looked back, as if to find me there. I sensed a smile come to her lips then. When the phone rang and she answered it to find another attentive relative I was with her, and she told them confidently that she was fine, and would be fine. Though they didn't believe it.

After a few weeks came our daughter's birthday. Laurie had a little party for her in the back yard. She invited her family and some of the children who lived on our street. At one moment, late in the afternoon, Laurie looked out the window to see Katie and her friends bumping about the yard in their bright dresses and party hats. Laurie's mother and sisters were out there too, as was my mother, and our close neighbors. Sunlight painted them all, and the treetops moved in a light wind. Laurie saw it all, as if from a seat in a movie theater, one without sound. She gathered the paper plates, forks, and napkins she had come to retrieve, but stopped to look out the kitchen window once again to catch another few seconds of the movie. I was there. I could hear her exhale gently as she said, *I'll be okay.*

From there I went straight to Katie.

Katie, when she was two, had been fond of the word *me.* Everything belonged to her, as did everyone. *Me-ball. Me-ma. Me-doll.* She had Laurie's determination coupled with my mother's quick wit. I loved that about her, even if I felt she never gave me her full attention. Kids are like that.

She was five years old when I died. She knew I was gone. When Laurie explained it to her she nodded quickly, asked a question or two, and was off. I no longer belonged to her. Now I see her wandering around the house, and even though she can speak properly, she repeats lightly to herself: *me- , me- , me- .*

Laurie was upstairs with Luke the day Katie decided to go down to the basement to find her old doll. The wooden steps in our house are strong, but there is no rail. *My doll,* she determinedly said, marching down those stairs in cadence. But her determination proved dangerous, because she missed a step half-way down and fell quickly over the side. I instinctively held out a hand and lifted her to safety, as surprised as she was at my agility. Children see things adults do not. She continued down the last steps and spotted her doll lying on the painted concrete. She locked in on its position and ran over to pick I up.

My Daddy, she said. That was our secret.

Luke was not much older than three when I died. He was not one to talk much. Laurie was worried he might never speak. We only had Katie to compare him to, and she had learned quickly. Luke just stared, sometimes raising his eyebrows so that you knew he understood you. But he saw no point in speaking.

We had spent many Saturday mornings together. The wheels were always turning in that little head of his, and by his eyes I could see that he had questions. His head spun one way then the other as he took in anything he saw or felt: a jet flying overhead, a bumblebee passing by, a strong wind. But he only pointed and made a little noise. I was always in the background, even then. And where Katie thought everything belonged to her, Luke was content, it seemed, to let everything be.

Once he wandered into the woods two lots away from our home, traveling through the neighbors' back yards to get there. I had been trying to put together a swing set, and cursing the fact that I didn't have the right tools. He must have run quickly to get there; I swear he had been under my watchful eye that morning.

My heart thumped so strongly I could feel it pressing on my lungs; I couldn't catch my breath. Where had he gone?

I checked all the familiar places first: the sloping side yards of our house, the thick stand of lilacs, the alley at the bottom of our long yard. Then I looked right, and noticed that you could walk straight to the woods through the other yards. There were no fences, no dogs, and no bushes in the way. I leapt over the grassy plots and made my way to the locust trees at the woods' edge. There was a path, well-worn by the older neighborhood kids, that welcomed me into the dense green.

I didn't have to go far, for he was sitting on a fallen tree trunk, playing with a large insect as it rolled around on his arm. My instinct was to shout, but Luke looked so content there. He smiled up at me and even laughed a little. What could I do? *No*, I said. For a moment he looked at me, genuinely perplexed. Then he began crying. I carried him home. By the time we reached our door he had his head on my shoulder, asleep.

A few days later, while at work, I got a phone call from Laurie. She spoke so loudly I had to hold the phone away from my ear.

—What? I said. What?

—He spoke!

—What did he say?

—He said, *Daddy come home?*

—Wow! From nothing to that?

—That's what he said.

—Guess I better come home then. I'll try not to be late.

It's not that I am more concerned with him than the others, but Luke was a puzzle I'll never be allowed to solve. He is already burning his own path, though I've noticed that faraway look in his eyes more often since I'm gone. I don't know how to reach him, how to slip under his skin the way I have with Laurie and Katie. I am both aware and unaware of the reason I must do this. It's just part of who I am right now.

Was there something I missed? For though time has ceased to exist for me, and I have leapt to another realm, I still do catch glimpses of them. I see that Laurie has remarried, and that Katie is as confidant and outspoken as ever.

I only cross paths with them when something—which I cannot name—is right, a convergence that occurs naturally between both our levels of existence. It comes as a surprise to both of us, and naturally afterwards we continue on our ways.

What I missed was all the keys that would unlock my son. I don't know where they came from, who gifted them or dropped them in his path. All I see is that he is now a man. He has borne his own children, taken turns that have left their scars. Yet in spite of what he has survived, he still wears that distant gaze. I see it through the dawn, when we sometimes meet in dreams. I feel he has broken through the barriers more than once. I sense this is dangerous for him, and I strain to feel it from his side.

I imagine what he might have come to be if I hadn't died. His gaze might have surrendered to a happy boyhood, full of healthy distractions and cutting rituals which he would have accepted freely. But what happened was that he accepted nothing freely; every trial was measured against my departure and deemed less important. It was a path he traveled without a nod to others, without help, without acknowledgement of the ways of the world. For that world broke all the rules for him, and he found no guidance to navigate its broken path.

The only consolation I can find is that he uses his uncommon perspective to bring light to others who may have found themselves in the same circumstance. He is not judgmental; nor does he expect any normalcy in the situations life dishes up. His easy-going nature is itself a comfort to everyone. And I feel I am still connected through him to that world I left so long ago. I am in his frozen gaze; I am in his words, whether spoken or written. That is our private victory.

For he has written these words too.

About the Author

Mark Saba grew up in Pittsburgh. He is the author of *The Landscapes of Pater* (fiction) and two collections of poetry, *Painting a Disappearing Canvas* and *Calling the Names,* as well as several other fiction ebooks available from Smashwords. His fiction, poetry, and creative nonfiction have appeared in literary magazines and anthologies around the U.S. and abroad. He is a graduate of Wesleyan University and Hollins University. Also a visual artist, he has created oil paintings and poetry videos, and is a graphic designer and medical illustrator at Yale University. Visit him at *www.marksabawriter.com.*